FALLEN ANGEL

A DERRICK ANDERSON ADVENTURE

MATTHEW GUNNOE

TWISTED SKIES
PUBLISHING

Fallen Angel: A Derrick Anderson Adventure
Copyright ©2025 Twisted Skies Publishing

Icon has been designed using images from Flaticon.com

Cover has been designed using images from Canva.com

Trade Paperback ISBN: 979-8-9903356-7-7

Published by Twisted Skies Publishing
Wichita, KS 67220

https://www.twistedskiespublishing.com

DEDICATION

To my wife,

Your unwavering love, patience, and belief in me
make every word possible.

This story, like so much in my life, is better because
of you. Thank you for being my greatest adventure
and my safest harbor.

CHAPTER 1

The Blackhawk's rotors sliced through the evening air, whipping up a storm of leaves and dirt as it roared over CIA headquarters. Derrick squinted against the chaos, his shirt tugging in the gusts while the sharp tang of jet fuel filled his nose. Lydia turned, holding Madeline close to shield her from the swirling debris.

When the helicopter landed, the door slid open with a metallic groan. Derrick gestured for Lydia to climb in. "Go on," he urged over the engine's roar. "I've got her," taking Madeline from her arms.

Lydia scrambled into the cabin, and Derrick followed, hoisting himself up one-handed while holding Madeline securely against his chest. Tae climbed in last, pulling the door shut with a sharp clang.

A crew member passed Derrick a headset, which he carefully slipped over Madeline's ears before putting on his own. The deafening thunder of the rotors dulled to a manageable hum, replaced by the soft crackle of voices over the comms.

Madeline clung tightly to his arm as the helicopter jolted into the air. She buried her face in his side, her small hands clutching the fabric of his jacket. "Hang on, kiddo," Derrick told her, gently stroking her back.

Lydia glanced out the window, the tension in her shoulders easing as they leveled out. Below them, D.C.'s lights stretched out like a shimmering map. The Lincoln Memorial stood stoic in the glow, and the Washington Monument's long shadow reached across the Mall. Even Madeline peeked up for a moment, her wide eyes drawn to the twinkling scene.

Tae leaned toward Derrick and tapped his shoulder. "You have any idea what this is about?"

"Not really," Derrick said, adjusting his headset.

Tae frowned, his voice dropping slightly. "The President's daughter was kidnapped less than an hour ago."

Derrick's gaze drifted outside as the name stirred uneasy memories. "Operation Lord Kenboat," he whispered quietly.

Tae raised an eyebrow. "You mean that's a real thing? Sounds like something a bored intern made up during lunch."

"It's an old exercise," Derrick said. "Kidnap a high-value target, demand ransom, watch the chaos unfold. We ran it on paper—never thought we'd see it for real."

Tae rubbed his face. "Let's hope our plan's not as dumb as that name."

The helicopter banked sharply, circling the White House before descending toward the South

Lawn. The cabin rattled violently as the aircraft touched down, the rotors thrashing the air like a tornado twisting overhead.

The doors opened and Lydia jumped down, her heels sinking slightly into the damp grass. Derrick handed Madeline to her before following, landing with a grunt. Tae was right behind, his eyes scanning the perimeter out of habit.

"This way!" yelled a Secret Service agent as he motioned toward the building.

The agent led them across the damp lawn, their steps muted by the rain-soaked grass. Madeline's wide eyes fixated on the massive structure ahead, its illuminated facade glowing against the twilight sky.

Inside the White House, the rumble of the helicopter faded to a faint hum, replaced by the heavy silence of sterile hallways. The air seemed denser, every step echoing as the group moved swiftly through the labyrinth of corridors.

"This looks familiar," Tae muttered, shooting Derrick a sidelong glance.

The secured door swung open to reveal the Situation Room, buzzing with controlled chaos. Aides hovered over glowing monitors while deep in conversations on their phones. At the center of it all stood President Habatian Green, his commanding presence undercut by the storm of worry etched into his furrowed brow. Beside him, Katherine's trembling hands clutched a tissue, her pale face streaked with tears.

Habatian stepped forward, offering Derrick a firm handshake. "Thank you for coming," he said, his voice steady, though the strain was unmistakable.

"We're at your service, sir. How can we help?" Derrick asked, meeting his gaze.

"Call me Habatian," the President said with a wave of dismissal. This was no time for formalities.

Before Derrick could respond, Katherine moved toward Lydia, pulling her into a desperate hug. Both women broke into quiet sobs, their shared fear spilling over in the dim room. Derrick glanced at Tae, who gave him a grim nod. This wasn't going to be just another mission.

"Let's sit," Habatian said, gesturing toward the table. His voice grew heavier as he began. "Katherine and Arabella were at soccer practice earlier this evening. Everything was normal—until three vans pulled into the lot."

Katherine's hands tightened into fists, the tissue crumpling under her grip.

"Armed men," Habatian continued. "Coordinated, precise. They opened fire, grabbed Arabella, and were gone before the Secret Service could mount a proper response. The agents did what they could, but there were too many civilians to risk a direct confrontation. By the time they engaged, the vans had split up. Arabella's vanished."

The room fell into a heavy silence. Tae leaned forward, breaking it. "What's her codename?"

"Angel," an officer replied without hesitation.

Derrick's fingers drummed against the table. "The new op name is *Fallen Angel* then."

Tae sighed and mumbled to himself. "Oh, thank goodness we don't have to use the other one."

After shooting Tae a side glance, he said, "First step: lock down every airport in the area—Dulles, Reagan, Baltimore. Check the ports, too. Nothing gets out unnoticed."

"We've done all that," Habatian said, frustration creeping into his voice. "There's nothing."

"What about Richmond?" Tae asked sharply. "Did anyone check Richmond International?"

The President froze, his eyes narrowing. "Richmond..." He turned to an aide. "Get TSA on the line. Now."

The aide bolted, returning moments later with a phone. Habatian barked orders into the receiver. "Lock down Richmond. Every gate. Stop every outbound flight."

The tension in the room thickened as they waited. The phone rang again, and the President switched it to speaker.

"Richmond's sealed, sir, but a private jet is already taxiing. They're not responding to communications."

Derrick's stomach dropped. "The ground stop might've just cleared the way for them."

"Stop that plane," Habatian ordered, his voice edged with steel.

The screen flickered to live footage of the jet barreling down the runway, pursued by flashing police cars. Sirens wailed, adding to the chaos. Derrick's fists clenched as the plane surged ahead, the blockade at the end of the runway drawing closer.

"It's not slowing down," an aide reported, his voice tight.

The jet roared past the blockade, its wheels lifting off the ground at the last possible second. The gust from its takeoff scattered debris and sent officers staggering back as the plane disappeared into the night sky.

Habatian slammed his fist on the table, the sound echoing through the room and muffling the curse he screamed out in frustration. "Scramble fighters!" he barked. "And find that plane!"

Seconds later, the grim report came through. "Sir, the transponder's offline."

Arabella was gone.

The room sank into silence, the weight of the failure pressing down on everyone. Derrick's gaze shifted toward Lydia, who stood by the door, Madeline resting on her hip. Her shoulders were rigid, her worry evident in the way her eyes lingered on him. She carried a worry he didn't need words to understand.

Lydia turned her attention to Katherine, who remained frozen in place, her hands trembling. Without a word, Lydia placed a hand on her arm and gently guided her—and Madeline—toward the door, giving them both a moment away from the suffocating tension of the room.

***

They entered the sitting area of the Presidential living quarters, where the warm glow of lamplight attempted to soften the weight of the moment. The plush chairs arranged around the room seemed designed to comfort, but they couldn't quite touch the tension hanging in the air. Katherine gave a brief, shaky wave to the Secret Service agents, who silently exited, taking up their posts outside the door. The heavy click of the latch closing marked a shift as the room suddenly became quieter and more intimate.

Lydia gently guided Katherine to a chair and knelt beside her. "How are you holding up?" she asked softly.

Katherine pressed trembling fingers to her cheeks, swiping at tears that came faster than she could stop. Her voice broke as she spoke, each word weighted with guilt. "I should have known better," she whispered. "All she wanted was to feel normal—just a kid playing soccer with her friends."

Her hands clenched tightly in her lap as her gaze dropped to the floor. "Habatian and I said no for so long. We thought about the security risks, the attention it would draw... everything. But she begged. She wanted it so badly, and I thought—" Her voice cracked again as she shook her head. "I thought it was safe. I thought it was enough."

Her shoulders trembled, and when the words came again, they were uneven, broken by quiet sobs. "I let her down."

Lydia didn't interrupt. She stayed quiet, offering a steadying presence and giving Katherine the space to let it all out.

"Arabella loved soccer," Katherine continued after a moment, her voice thin and raw. "She begged me for months to let her play. And finally, I gave in. I thought if we kept it simple—just a couple of plainclothes agents, no motorcade, nothing flashy—it would be fine. She could just... be a kid for once." She pressed her fingers to her lips, her shoulders shaking as tears spilled over again. "But it wasn't enough. It wasn't safe."

The dam broke completely. Katherine buried her face in her hands, her sobs unrestrained now, guilt spilling over in waves. Lydia reached out and rested a hand on her shoulder, giving it a reassuring squeeze.

"Katherine," she began softly, "I remember when Derrick and I brought Madeline here for the Easter egg roll. Arabella and Madeline were inseparable that day. They ran all over the lawn like they'd known each other their whole lives. It was complete chaos."

A small, shaky laugh escaped Katherine between her tears. "They were, weren't they?" she whispered, her voice trembling but lighter. "She was so happy that day. I hadn't seen her smile like that in months."

"That's who she is," Lydia said gently, leaning closer. "She's strong, Katherine. She's going to make it through this. I know you're scared—I would be too—but Derrick will stop at nothing to bring her home. I promise you, she'll be safe."

For a moment, Katherine just stared at Lydia, her red-rimmed eyes searching for reassurance. Slowly, she reached out and gripped Lydia's hand tightly, holding on as though it were the only thing keeping her steady. "I hope you're right," she murmured, barely audible. "I don't know what I'd do if—"

"Don't," Lydia said firmly, cutting her off. "Don't go there. Arabella's coming back. Derrick will bring her home."

Katherine nodded, swallowing hard, her grip on Lydia's hand loosening slightly. The fear hadn't left her, but Lydia's unwavering conviction was enough to keep her from unraveling. For now, that had to be enough.

***

Back in the Situation Room, the atmosphere was suffocating, heavy with tension and the relentless hum of unanswered questions. Phones rang constantly, aides speaking in clipped, hurried tones as they chased leads that seemed to evaporate as quickly as they formed. Around the room, screens flickered with satellite feeds, flight paths, and live news reports—an overwhelming torrent of information, yet none of it provided a clear answer.

Derrick sat at the edge of the table, elbows on his knees, his eyes glued to the looping footage of the jet's takeoff. He hit rewind again for what felt like the hundredth time, narrowing his focus on the tail of the plane. The numbers there were distorted, obscured by poor lighting and the camera's low resolution.

"Come on..." he muttered under his breath, leaning closer. His finger hovered over the zoom control, his frustration mounting as the image refused to sharpen.

Frame by frame, he worked, his eyes straining against the blur. A flicker—a hint of clarity—caught his attention. The first character sharpened slightly: Z. Derrick straightened, his pulse quickening. Adjusting the contrast, he pressed forward. Another letter emerged: X.

He rewound the footage again, this time moving even slower. The final digits became barely readable: 61.

The sounds of the room—the ringing phones, hurried voices, the hum of equipment—faded into the background, drowned out by the singular focus of his stare on the screen. For a moment, it was just him and the grainy image. He leaned back slightly, before calling out, "Nordlithia!" The room fell into silence.

Heads turned sharply, and President Habatian lowered the phone from his ear, his expression sharp and questioning. "What did you say?"

Derrick pointed at the screen. "That plane—it's registered in Nordlithia."

The name dropped like a stone into a calm pond, rippling through the room. Conversations halted, and an uneasy stillness took hold as the significance sank in.

Habatian's jaw clenched. "Get me everything we have on Nordlithia," he barked, turning toward one of his aides. "Now!"

The room erupted into motion as aides scrambled for reports, maps, and intelligence on the isolated nation. Papers shuffled, phones buzzed, and voices murmured in tense exchanges, but Derrick stayed still, leaning back in his chair with arms crossed, his eyes fixed on the screen where the plane's shadow melted into the night.

Tae stood beside him, rubbing his jaw as he spoke. "Nordlithia," he muttered, the word rolling off his tongue like something bitter. "That's... near Norway, right? Freezing cold?"

Derrick nodded, his gaze never leaving the screen. "Cold, remote, and practically locked down. It's wilderness—dense forests, cliffs that drop straight into freezing water, mountains so jagged they look carved by knives."

The President, now holding a detailed map handed to him by an aide, turned to Derrick, his expression grim. "You're saying they took her to the middle of nowhere?"

"It's worse than that," Derrick said, his voice low and steady. "The government there controls everything. One airport, with no flights in or out without their approval. Outsiders don't just waltz in, especially not Americans."

Habatian's eyes narrowed. "What kind of government are we talking about?"

"That's the thing," Derrick said, briefly meeting Tae's gaze. "Nobody really knows. The place is a black hole. The rumors range from shadowy powerbrokers to rogue military operatives pulling the strings. They've been stonewalling the U.S. for decades—no diplomacy, no transparency."

Tae let out a slow whistle. "Sounds like the setup to a bad spy novel."

Derrick's tone darkened. "It gets worse. If that jet landed there, this isn't just a kidnapping. It's calculated—a move meant to bait us."

The President stiffened, his hand gripping the map tighter. "You're saying this isn't about Arabella?"

Derrick's gaze dropped, his voice grim. "Not entirely. It's a message."

CHAPTER 2

The steady hum of the C32-A's engines filled the cabin as the plane climbed away from Andrews Air Force Base, bound for Norway. Hunched over his laptop, Derrick's fingers flew across the keyboard, scrolling through flight-tracking websites and combing through data. Every lead so far had evaporated, leaving his frustration simmering beneath a calm exterior.

Across the aisle, Jack Raines methodically cleaned his weapon, each movement slow and deliberate, the mark of someone who'd done this countless times. Rebecca "Becky" Lawson, leaning back with her arms crossed, watched Derrick with a casual sharpness. Her laid-back demeanor masked the kind of confidence that came from surviving more than a few close calls.

"So," Becky said, her tone light, "is that laptop going to crack the case, or just melt your brain?"

"Right now?" Derrick smirked without looking up. "It's leaning toward the latter."

Jack chuckled quietly as he set the gun aside. "Sometimes you've got to trust your gut. Technology's great, but instincts'll take you further."

"Or get you into trouble," Becky teased, nudging him with her elbow. "Don't listen to him,

Derrick. Jack thinks the world's problems can be solved with a gut feeling and a Glock."

"Hey, works often enough," Jack shot back with a shrug. His gaze flicked toward Derrick's hands, where faint scars trailed up his forearms. He tilted his head thoughtfully. "Looks like you've had your share of close calls."

The words hit Derrick like a jolt, dragging him into a memory he'd rather forget. The cabin dimmed in his mind, replaced by the cold, suffocating light of a grimy motel room. A blade pressed into his wrists, slow and deliberate, as Izzy's mocking grin loomed over him. The phantom sting burned anew, and his breath caught in his throat.

A firm hand then landed on his shoulder. "Derrick." Tae's voice cut through the fog, snapping him back to the present.

He blinked, the cabin coming into focus again as he drew a steadying breath. "Yeah," he replied, clearing his throat. "I'm good."

Jack didn't push, though his gaze lingered, silently acknowledging the weight of whatever history Derrick carried. "I'd take you on my side any day," he said simply.

"Let's keep him in one piece first," Becky interjected, nudging Jack with a grin. "We're going to need him at full capacity."

Tae, now seated beside Derrick in tactical gear, leaned closer. "Any luck?"

"None," Derrick replied under his breath, shaking his head. "It's like the plane vanished."

"What about the tail number?" Becky asked, leaning forward.

"It's registered to a shell company in Nordlithia," he said with a frustrated sigh. "Flimsy lead, but it's all we've got."

"Folding his hands, Jack spoke in a low voice. 'Nordlithia's a tough nut to crack. If that's where they've taken her, we're not getting her back without a fight.'"

"Assuming that's where they're headed," Tae added.

Derrick leaned back in his chair, crossing his arms. "We don't know for sure. That's the problem."

Becky stretched and rolled her neck until it cracked. "Flimsy leads are still leads. We've worked with less and pulled through. We'll figure it out." She grinned. "Don't sweat it too much, Anderson."

"She's right," Jack added. "We've got skills, and we've got time. It's not the worst position to be in."

Derrick closed his laptop with a sigh, letting the words linger in his mind. Their confidence wasn't bravado—it came from experience. But this mission felt different. The stakes were higher, the risks sharper, and the margin for error razor-thin.

"You realize we're walking straight into a lion's den, right? Either of you been to Nordlithia before?" Tae asked, leaning back in his chair.

"Once," Becky replied, "Protection detail. Let's just say it wasn't exactly a warm welcome. The place is freezing, the terrain's unforgiving, and the locals? They hate outsiders."

"That's putting it mildly," Jack added. "You don't go there expecting a cakewalk. But hey, we've faced worse.

"Fair enough," Tae said, settling back into his seat.

Kicking her feet up, Becky smirked. "Long flight ahead, boys. Might as well enjoy the peace while it lasts."

Derrick chuckled, shaking his head. "Are you two always this laid back?"

"Stress kills," Becky said with a grin. "Save the worrying for when the bullets fly."

Jack leaned back, his tone easing. "Pacing yourself is half the battle. You learn when to gear up and when to conserve energy."

"That wisdom or just experience?" Tae asked, raising an eyebrow.

Derrick glanced out the window at the dark expanse of sky, a flicker of Lydia's face flashing in his mind. Her smile and warmth calmed his soul.

Turning back, he sighed. "Alright. You win. But if this goes sideways, I'm holding you to that 'gut feeling.'"

Jack chuckled. "It hasn't failed me yet."

Becky grinned. "And when it does, I'll be there to clean up the mess."

The plane jolted suddenly, shaking the overhead compartments. Becky barely looked up, smirking as she tightened the strap on her vest. "If we go down, I call dibs on the inflatable raft."

***

The morning light barely touched the horizon as the plane's wheels touched down smoothly on the runway in Oslo. Derrick stood and stretched, trying to shake off the stiffness from hours of sitting. Nearby, Tae was already pulling his bag from the overhead compartment, while Jack and Becky packed their gear.

At the bottom of the stairs, a group of Norwegian officials stood waiting. Dressed in dark suits, they looked professional but carried a noticeable edge of unease. One man, tall and broad-shouldered, clutched a clipboard under his arm. His eyes tracked their luggage with just a little too much focus, lingering on the bags longer than necessary.

"This is where it gets tricky," Derrick muttered as they descended the steps, the brisk morning air waking him up faster than coffee.

The man with the clipboard stepped forward, giving a curt nod. "Welcome to Oslo. I understand you're here on a sensitive mission, but we'll need to discuss the weapons you're carrying."

"We're here on official business, authorized by the President of the United States," Jack said in a stern voice. "All the clearances should be in order."

The official didn't budge. "Norwegian regulations regarding firearms are very strict, even for foreign agents. I'm afraid we'll need to confiscate your weapons until further notice."

Becky cast a sideways glance at Derrick. "Told you it wouldn't be easy," she quipped.

"Hang tight," Derrick sighed, pulling out his phone.

Becky, on the other hand, looked completely unbothered, her gaze wandering casually across the tarmac like she had all the time in the world.

After a few rings, President Green's voice came through the line. "Derrick? You made it?"

"Yeah, but we've hit a snag," Derrick said, glancing at the official. "They're not thrilled about the hardware we brought. Think you could smooth this over?"

There was a brief pause on the other end, followed by a weary sigh. "Hold on. I'll see what I can do."

The man with the clipboard raised an eyebrow, his patience visibly wearing thin. Derrick offered a polite smile, stalling as best he could. The tension hung in the chilly air until Derrick's phone buzzed again. This time, the incoming call wasn't from Green—it was from a Norwegian official.

At the same moment, the official's phone rang. He answered, exchanged a few clipped words in Norwegian, and then turned back to the group. His tone had softened, but a note of warning lingered. "It seems you've been granted special permission by the President of Norway himself. You may proceed with your weapons, but your activities will be closely monitored."

Derrick nodded, feeling some of the tension ease. "Understood. We won't be here long."

Slinging his bag over his shoulder, Jack nodded toward the pairs of SUVs nearby. "Let's get moving."

Gravel crunched under the tires as the SUVs rolled to a stop near the water's edge. The low rumble of the engines faded, leaving only the faint lapping of waves against the rocky shore. In the distance, shrouded by the dimming light, Nordlithia's coastline loomed like a ghost on the horizon. The sun dipped lower, stretching shadows across the ground and reminding them they had only a few hours before darkness swallowed everything.

The air carried a faint chill, the kind that hinted at colder winds waiting just beyond nightfall. Derrick stepped out and scanned the area. His boots sank into the damp ground slightly as he took in the quiet isolation of the shoreline. No lights, no movement—nothing to give away their presence. Even the sea looked eerily calm, its glassy surface betraying none of the chaos it could unleash without warning.

"Alright," Derrick called out. "Let's get to it."

The team sprang into action, unloading the Zodiacs from the backs of the SUVs. The quiet gave way to the low hum of electric pumps as the boats slowly took shape, their rubber shells inflating. Tae knelt beside one of the boats, securing the valves. He glanced up in time to see Derrick slipping two small canisters into his vest.

"Seriously, phosphamite?" Tae groaned, rolling his eyes. "One stray bullet, and we'll be headlining international news."

Derrick didn't even look up. "It's just a precaution."

"Right," Tae said under his breath, zipping up his pack. "That's what you always say. Just try not to turn this into a fireworks show unless it's absolutely necessary."

A faint smirk tugged at Derrick's lips. "When hasn't it been necessary?"

Tae rolled his eyes again, giving Derrick a light nudge as he passed. "I'm keeping count, you know."

The last traces of sunlight faded, leaving the shore shrouded in a pale gray twilight. The air grew sharper and colder as they dragged the inflated Zodiacs toward the water. Soft scraping sounds filled the stillness as the rubber hulls slid across the rocky beach.

Derrick stopped mid-step, his head tilting as he caught something—a faint, rhythmic thump carried by the wind. It was low, barely audible, but persistent, like the distant beat of a drum. His pulse quickened as he scanned the horizon.

"What is it?" Tae asked, noticing Derrick's hesitation.

Derrick squinted, looking into the distance. "Thought I heard something. Like... a drum. Or maybe footsteps."

Tae paused, listening, then shrugged with a smirk. "Sure it's not your nerves kicking in?"

"I know what I heard," Derrick replied, glancing toward the distant coastline. His voice lowered. "And I saw something—just for a second. A flicker of light. Could've been a reflection."

Tae's grin widened as he raised an eyebrow. "Ghosts, huh? Maybe Nordlithia's haunted."

"Just stay focused."

"Relax," Tae said, giving him a playful nudge. "But if something crawls out of the water, you're taking the lead."

Derrick adjusted his gear as he continued to scan the horizon. The sound was gone now, and the light was nowhere to be seen. Still, the unease clung to him, refusing to let go.

Derrick stepped out into the frigid waters and steadied the boat for Tae to get in. Once he was settled, Derrick climbed in after, taking up his position by the engine. A glance over his shoulder confirmed Becky and Jack were doing the same.

Settling into her seat, Becky's gaze flicked to the darkening horizon. The jagged silhouette of Nordlithia barely visible now. "It's going to get pitch-black out there fast," she said with concern.

"That's the idea," Jack replied. "Harder to spot us in the dark."

Glancing at the others, Derrick reminded them of the plan. "Stay close. Keep it quiet. We move fast— get in, get out."

The engines then purred to life as the Zodiacs slowly glided forward.

The wind hit sharply against their faces, colder now that they were moving. The salty tang of the sea mixed with the exhaust of the motors, whose sound was almost drowned out by the rush of water against the hulls. Ahead, Nordlithia's shadowy coastline loomed closer, rising out of the sea like a jagged sentinel.

Becky's voice crackled over the radio. "Looks quiet so far. Let's hope it stays that way."

Derrick didn't answer, his eyes fixed on the approaching shore. The uneasy weight in his chest grew heavier with every second, but he pushed it aside. There was no room for doubt, no time for second-guessing.

The shoreline's features sharpened as they drew closer revealing jagged cliffs and a small, narrow beach where they could make landfall.

No alarms. No lights. Just the cold, creeping tension of knowing that the hard part hadn't even begun.

CHAPTER 3

The boats drifted silently to a stop on the beach. Faint moonlight filtered through the clouds, offering just enough light to reveal the vague outlines of trees a few feet ahead. The air was sharp and cold, biting through their jackets as the team worked quickly, securing the Zodiacs and unloading their gear.

Derrick scanned the shoreline. The quiet felt oppressive with every small sound amplified in the stillness. "No turning back now," he whispered, adjusting his gear and hefting his pack.

"It's going to be a long hike," Tae replied quietly, patting Derrick on the back.

They set off up the hillside, where they found a small path that would lead them through the ten miles of unforgiving, rocky terrain.

The cold was relentless. With each breath, small clouds formed in front of their faces, fading quickly into the night. Tae, Jack, and Becky moved ahead with ease, their strides smooth and unbroken. Derrick, on the other hand, felt the strain creeping into his legs as the miles dragged on, each step reminding him just how long it had been since he'd done this kind of work. He lagged behind slightly, his breath coming heavier, muscles burning.

A glance over the shoulder confirmed what Tae already knew. He slowed just enough to toss a grin Derrick's way. "Getting slow on me, old man?"

"Just pacing myself," Derrick shot back, not bothering to hide the effort in his voice.

From up front, Becky's quiet laugh carried through the still air. "You better keep up, Anderson. Fall behind and we'll leave you here."

Derrick snorted, "You'd miss me too much, and you know it!"

By the time they reached the edge of the airport, Derrick's legs felt like lead. Sweat trickled down his back despite the biting cold, his breaths heavy and uneven. Tae, Jack, and Becky seemed unfazed by the trek, showing no signs of slowing down.

Jack knelt at the base of the chain-link fence, pulling out a tool from his pack. A quiet snip of wire cutters broke the silence as he worked quickly, forming a clean hole large enough to crawl through. "We're in," he whispered, motioning for the others to follow.

One by one, they slipped through the opening, staying low as they disappeared into the shadows. The airport stretched out ahead, eerily quiet under the faint glow of a few scattered lights. Several parked planes stood in the distance, their shadows stretching across the tarmac. Derrick crouched low behind a stack of equipment, his breath puffing into the cold night air as he scanned the tarmac for movement.

A faint sound broke the stillness—muffled voices, distant but clear enough to catch his attention. Tae shifted slightly, glancing over at Derrick. "You hear that?" he whispered.

Derrick nodded, motioning toward the sound. "Voices. Far side."

Becky moved closer, straining to listen. "Could be guards," she whispered. "Too quiet to tell."

A flicker of light cut through the darkness, sweeping briefly across the far side of the runway. Derrick stiffened, following the beam as it vanished just as quickly as it had appeared.

"Flashlights," he muttered. "They're moving."

Tae nodded grimly. "They're patrolling. Small group, by the sound of it."

The team froze, holding their breath as the seconds dragged on. The voices grew louder briefly before fading into the silence of the sprawling airport. The light didn't return.

"Clear?" Becky whispered.

"Clear enough," Derrick replied quietly. "Let's move."

They crept forward, staying low. When they reached the hangars, each slipped into position and began searching for the plane.

When they regrouped minutes later, Derrick's frustration was clear. "Nothing. If it's not here, we'll have to check that shell company downtown. Might be the only lead we've got left."

Jack nodded, his eyes scanning the stillness around them. "Agreed. We can—"

A sudden flash of light swept across the tarmac, landing squarely on Jack's watch. The metallic gleam seemed blindingly bright in the dark.

"Move!" Derrick hissed, his heart already racing as a voice barked orders in Nordlithian.

The guard's voice rose behind them, joined by the sound of hurried footsteps and the erratic sweep of more flashlights. The team darted toward the far end of the airport, trying to avoid the beams of light cutting through the dark.

Jack reached the fence first, pulling out his wire cutters again as he dropped to a crouch. "Keep them off me," he said, working quickly.

Tae and Becky took up positions, scanning the open space behind them while Derrick crouched nearby, heart hammering as he watched the shifting lights.

"Almost there," Jack whispered, his voice tense. A few agonizing seconds later, he yanked the cut section aside. "Go, go, go!"

One by one, they scrambled through the opening just as the guards rounded the corner, their shouts growing louder. Jack pulled the fence back into place, securing it enough to slow anyone coming after them.

They ducked behind a nearby hill, crouching low as they caught their breath. Derrick's chest heaved as he wiped the sweat from his face. "Way too close," he wheezed, glancing back toward the airport.

Tae, still breathing steady, flashed him a grin. "Good thing you paced yourself, huh?"

Derrick shook his head, managing a tired laugh. "Let's just get out of here. I'd rather not see those guys again."

The early morning hours draped Skjolvik in a strange quiet as the capital's streets were nearly deserted under the dim, flickering glow of streetlights. Their pale light reflected off the occasional passing car or the shuffle of a lone pedestrian, but otherwise, the city felt like it was holding its breath. Moving around the outskirts had been one thing. Here, in the heart of the city, sticking out would surely get them caught.

At the edge of a shadowy alley, Derrick studied the street ahead. The address tied to the shell company was buried deep in Skjolvik's business district, where sneaking around as they had earlier wasn't an option. They needed a plan.

Tae stepped up beside him, voice low. "We can't just stroll in there. Tactical gear doesn't exactly scream 'locals out for a morning jog.'"

In the lot ahead, a beat-up Nissan Leaf sat alone, its light blue paint dulled by grime. Derrick's eyes lingered on it before a grin tugged at the corner of his mouth. "I've got an idea."

Becky followed his gaze and let out a short laugh. "A Leaf? You're kidding."

"It's electric," Derrick said, already heading toward it. "Quiet. Inconspicuous. No one's going to expect four armed operatives rolling up in one of these."

He crouched beside the car, knife in hand. A few quick moves and the lock popped open. The door creaked slightly as he swung it wide, and a satisfied smirk crossed his face. "Piece of cake."

Jack didn't even try to hide his amusement as he loaded their bags into the trunk. "You've got some weird skills, Anderson."

A bit of fiddling with the wires, and the car hummed softly to life. Derrick slid into the driver's seat as the others piled in behind him.

Tae pulled the door shut, glancing out the window. "Let's hope we don't end up in a high-speed chase."

"Relax," Derrick said, his tone dry. "I'll give them a head start."

The Leaf wasn't fast, but it did the job, humming quietly as it rolled past rows of shuttered buildings under the dim glow of streetlights. Derrick kept a steady grip on the wheel, his eyes scanning the alleys and storefronts. Every shadow seemed to stretch longer than it should, every flicker of movement tugging at his focus.

In the back seat, Jack shifted uncomfortably, his head brushing the roof every time the car hit a bump. "This thing's built for kids, not grown men," he grumbled, wedging his knees against the seat in front of him.

Tae glanced back, grinning. "This car's eco-friendly, not Sasquatch-friendly. Blame the planet."

The minutes dragged on as tension grew with each turn. Finally, after what felt like hours, they reached their destination—a squat, unmarked warehouse sandwiched between two drab office buildings. Its dark exterior gave away nothing, blending seamlessly into the lifeless surroundings.

Derrick brought the Leaf to a stop and cut off the engine. Jack grumbled from the back seat, wedging himself out with a mix of awkward angles and muttered curses. "Next time, I'm calling shotgun," he growled, stretching his legs once he was free.

Grabbing his lockpick, Jack moved to the door. The faint scrape of metal against metal cut through the stillness until the lock clicked open. "We're in," he whispered.

The air inside the warehouse was stale, thick with the smell of dust and old machinery. Derrick flicked on a small flashlight, keeping the beam low as he scanned the room. His steps seemed to echo louder than they should as he walked among rows of rusted equipment.

"Split up," he whispered, motioning to Tae and Jack. "Keep it quiet."

Derrick and Becky moved carefully, their boots scraping lightly against the concrete as they approached a desk shoved against the far wall. Papers were scattered across it, curling with age, but something caught Derrick's eye—a folder with fresh ink smudges along the edge.

He opened it, flipping through quickly. Maintenance records, shipping manifests, and hangar rentals. All were in Nordlithia… except for one. Derrick studied the outlier for a moment. "Astana, Kazakhstan," he whispered as he tapped the page. "What are you hiding?"

A faint rustling noise stopped him cold. He held his breath, his ears straining. From the far corner of the warehouse came the soft creak of something shifting, like a weight pressing on the floorboards. His flashlight snapped in that direction, but the space was empty.

Tae's voice made him jump as it crackled over the comms. "Find anything?"

Derrick exhaled slowly, catching his breath. "Hangar listings. One in Astana."

"Has promise. Keep looking," Tae replied. "We'll check the far side."

As Derrick snapped a photo of the documents, his foot brushed against a small metal box on the floor. A low, mechanical *click* followed. He froze, his blood running cold.

"What was that?" Becky whispered sharply from across the room.

"Not good," Derrick muttered, glancing down. A small red light on the box flashed twice, then went steady. His stomach dropped. "We've got a problem."

A piercing alarm shattered the stillness as it echoed through the warehouse.

The group regrouped at the door, only to freeze as they pushed it open. Derrick's heart pounded as he scanned the lot, counting the soldiers spilling from the vehicles. Too many. His mind raced, weighing their options—none of them good.

"Nice touch with the alarm," Tae said, his voice dripping with sarcasm. "Really sets the mood for an escape, don't you think?"

"We're not walking out of this one," Derrick groaned, his mind racing. "Tae, any ideas?"

Tae's eyes darted over the scene, his frown deepening. "Not unless you've got a magic wand. We're boxed in."

Pulling the vial free, Derrick held it up just enough for Tae to see. The liquid inside shimmered faintly under the dim light. "Plan B," he said flatly.

"You're not serious..." Tae hissed, his voice dropping to a sharp whisper.

Becky stepped closer, her brow furrowed. "What is that?" she asked, her voice low but sharp.

Tae shot her a look, his tone dry. "Phosphamite. The kind of thing that puts you on international watchlists—for life."

"It's this or get caught," Derrick shot back, already crouching beside the car. Placing the vial beneath it, he didn't look up as he added, "Run when I say."

Becky and Jack were already running as Derrick stood and drew his gun. He locked eyes on Tae and said, "Run!"

The sharp crack of the gunshot split the air as the bullet hit the vial dead center.

The explosion ripped through the lot with a deafening roar, the phosphamite igniting the car's lithium battery in a blinding flash. Heat and light surged outward, the blast scattering debris and forcing the soldiers to dive for cover. Flames consumed the car, sending a fireball into the night sky and shaking the ground beneath them.

They tore through the warehouse, the roar of the explosion behind them growing louder with each step. The fireball surged through the open door, its heat licking at their heels as Derrick pushed himself harder.

"Must go faster! Must go faster!" Derrick yelled, his voice strained.

Ahead of him, Tae was already pulling away, his stride unbroken. "I *am* going faster!" he shouted back, not bothering to look over his shoulder.

Derrick gritted his teeth, lungs burning as he tried to close the gap, the heat from the fireball a constant reminder that slowing down wasn't an option.

They tore through the alleys, weaving between buildings as chaos continued behind them. The roar of crumbling masonry rolled through the night, growing louder with each passing second. Derrick glanced over his shoulder, catching sight of several buildings collapsing into a heap, dust and debris billowing into the air.

He felt a sharp tug on his arm and Tae's voice cutting through the noise. "You know what happened to Lot's wife. Let's go!"

Derrick turned and pushed himself harder, forcing his legs to keep pace with the others.

The sound of shouts and the faint whine of sirens grew more distant with every turn. The adrenaline dulled the cold bite of the air as they ran, hearts pounding in sync with their rapid footsteps.

Jack's voice cut through the noise as they ran. "Are you seriously telling me you've been walking around with that in your vest?!"

Without breaking stride, Derrick shot back, "You should see what's in the other vial."

By the time they reached the shoreline, Derrick sank against a rock, struggling to catch his breath. Tae was already untying the Zodiacs while Jack and Becky loaded the gear.

Tae shot Derrick a sideways glance, the sarcasm in his expression saying more than words ever could. "Yeah, I'm pretty sure that explosion really won the Nordlithians over."

Derrick, still catching his breath, managed a tired grin. "Always happy to help. Besides, they don't know who we were."

Becky snorted as she climbed into the boat. "Maybe next time, tone down the fireworks?"

"No promises," Derrick said, pulling himself into the Zodiac with a groan.

The motor hummed to life as they pushed off, the water quickly swallowing the chaos they'd left behind.

***

The light from the TV flickered in the room as Lydia sat on the couch flanked by Katherine on one side and Madeline on the other. Dinner was over, and the air should have been calm, but her mind refused to settle.

Madeline, oblivious to the tension, nestled comfortably between them with her eyes glued to the screen. Lydia idly flipped through the channels, barely registering the images that flickered past. Her fingers moved automatically while her thoughts miles away.

A news report caught her attention. The anchor's somber tone broke through the background noise. "Still no leads on the President's daughter's kidnapping," he said.

Her stomach twisted, the unease tightening in her chest no matter how deeply she tried to breathe. Her fingers hesitated for a moment before she switched the channel, unwilling to let her thoughts spiral about Derrick being in the thick of it.

But the next image stopped her cold. The screen filled with footage of a massive explosion ripping through Nordlithia's streets. Smoke billowed into the air, swallowing Skjolvik's skyline. Emergency lights flashed as first responders scrambled through the rubble of three collapsed buildings. The devastation made her heart sink.

She buried her face in her hands, her thoughts racing.

Katherine leaned forward as the name on the screen sank in. "Nordlithia... isn't that where they were going?"

A sigh escaped Lydia's lips. "Yes."

***

Back at the Oslo airport, the team raced across the tarmac toward their waiting plane. The chaos of the night lingered in their minds, but there was no time to unpack it. As soon as they boarded, Derrick pulled out his phone and dialed the President's direct line.

The call connected on the first ring. "Derrick, what do you have?" President Green asked.

Derrick exhaled, steadying himself. "We hit the shell company. Found documents linking hangars in Nordlithia and one in Astana, Kazakhstan. It's not solid proof, but it's something."

The President was quiet for a moment before responding, "Alright. I'll work on getting you permission to enter Kazakhstan. Sit tight."

After what felt like an eternity, the President called back. "We've hit a snag. The Kazakh government won't allow an official U.S. op without definitive proof of Arabella's presence in the country. We don't have enough to convince them yet."

Derrick sighed, rubbing his temple. "Then we'll have to do it unofficially."

The President's tone softened, losing its usual formality. "Derrick, if you go that route, I can't help you. It has to be a full disavow. No ties to the U.S. government. If something goes wrong, it'll blow up in ways we can't contain. You understand what I'm saying, right?"

Derrick exhaled deeply, processing the implications. "I understand, sir. What about Jack and Becky? Can they come with us?"

"Negative," the President said firmly. "The Secret Service agents can't accompany you without official permission. And using the plane is out of the question as well. That thing is a billboard for the U.S."

Tae leaned forward, exchanging a look with Derrick before grabbing the phone. "Don't worry about it, Mr. President. I've got this."

Before the President could respond, Tae was already dialing another number. Within minutes, he had arranged for a CIA plane to meet them at the airport. Hanging up, he turned to Derrick with a triumphant grin. "Ride's on the way."

Derrick leaned against the stairs of the plane as the first slivers of morning light broke across the horizon.

Stepping up beside him, Tae blew soft clouds of breath into the crisp air. "Kazakhstan, huh?" he said, breaking the silence. "Not exactly a vacation spot. Think it'll be warmer?"

Derrick huffed a quiet laugh, though the tension didn't leave his face. "If they moved Arabella there, it's because they think it's safer. Harder for us to operate."

Tae nodded, pulling his jacket tighter. "Astana's a fortress. Big city, lots of eyes. Everyone's watching, and no one's friendly."

Derrick glanced at him. "You've worked there?"

"Once," Tae said, his voice low. "Enough to know we'll be walking into a maze. Surveillance is everywhere."

A faint whine of a jet engine drew their attention as the sleek Citation jet rolled toward them, its unmarked fuselage blending perfectly into the background. Derrick straightened, watching as it came to a stop, engines idling like a predator waiting to pounce.

Jack and Becky helped load the weapons and gear onto the smaller plane, double-checking everything before preparing to leave.

Extending his hand, Jack met Derrick's gaze. "Stay sharp out there. You two might be her last hope."

Becky offered a worrisome smile. "And do us all a favor—try not to blow anything else up unless it's absolutely necessary."

A soft chuckle escaped Derrick. "It's always necessary."

With their goodbyes said, Jack and Becky boarded their plane, heading back home. Derrick and Tae stood quietly, watching as the large jet disappeared into the sky, leaving only the faint outline of contrails against the rising sun.

Turning toward Derrick, Tae gestured to their new ride, grinning. "Final boarding call for Kazakhstan... all rows, all passengers."

CHAPTER 4

Clouds stretched endlessly below the plane in a vast, unbroken sea of white that seemed to blur into the horizon. Derrick stared out the window, his mind racing, trying to piece together a plan from the scraps of information they had. They were just a few hours away from landing in Astana, and the only thing guiding them was the hangar address they'd found. It wasn't much, but it was all they had.

Across from him, Tae sat fiddling absently with his phone. The cabin was silent until, finally, Tae spoke. "Why Kazakhstan? Of all places, why take her there?"

Leaning back, Derrick rubbed his eyes. "I've been wondering the same thing," he admitted. "Doesn't seem like the obvious choice, but if you're trying to disappear? It makes a strange kind of sense."

Tae nodded, his gaze drifting. "Smack in the middle of Russia and China... Just being near those two is enough to make anyone paranoid. You think they're planning to sell her off? Hand her over to one of them?"

The words hit hard. The thought wasn't new, but hearing it out loud made Derrick's stomach sink. "If this were about ransom, we'd have heard something by now. No demands, no communication... If it's not about money—"

"Then it's something worse," Tae said, finishing the thought. His voice dropped, heavy with the implications. "Someone with the power to keep her hidden. Or use her."

A tense silence filled the cabin. Tae frowned, looking out the window. "If that's the case, we're running out of time."

Astana came into view as the plane began its descent, the sprawling city a mix of gleaming skyscrapers and weathered remnants of its Soviet past. Beyond the city, endless plains stretched to the horizon making the modern skyline stand out even more.

Derrick's focus wasn't on the city, though. His attention stayed locked on the private hangars lining the edge of the airfield, scanning for what they'd come to find.

As their plane taxied down the runway, he saw a familiar silhouette. The aircraft they'd been searching for was parked in a private hangar.

"There it is," Derrick said, nudging Tae and motioning toward the building.

Tae leaned over, squinting as he took it in. "Looks like we've got the right place. Now the question is, how do we get in without setting off every alarm in this place?"

Derrick leaned back, a faint smirk crossing his face. "We're tourists. Couple of guys looking for a sightseeing flight. Wandered into the wrong hangar."

Tae stared at him, somewhere between disbelief and amusement. "That's the plan? Seriously? I'd rather kick the doors down."

"Let's try subtle first. If that doesn't work, we'll go loud."

Tae let out a soft laugh, shaking his head. "Alright, Mr. Tourist. I hope you're as charming as you think you are."

The plane rolled to a stop, and they moved quickly, carrying only what they needed to avoid drawing attention. Ahead, the hangar loomed, its plain exterior giving no hints about the secrets inside. Derrick ran through their cover story one last time—a pair of lost travelers stumbling into the wrong place. Just enough to buy them a moment to assess the situation.

As they reached the door, Derrick threw Tae a sidelong glance. "You ready for this?"

Tae flashed a grin, the mischief in his eyes unmistakable. "I was ready for this since kindergarten!"

Stepping into the hangar, the faint smell of jet fuel mingled with the metallic tang of machinery. Derrick kept his expression neutral, wearing his best "lost tourist" face. Behind him, Tae brushed a hand along the sleek surface of the wing, swaying slightly as if unsteady on his feet. "This..." he shouted, slurring his words for effect, "...this is a beautiful plane."

Three men turned at the commotion, their gazes darkening as they sized him up. Their expressions made it clear they weren't buying the act.

Derrick stepped forward, his tone apologetic. "Sorry about my idiot friend," he said, motioning toward Tae, who leaned heavily against the plane. "He thought this was one of those sightseeing places. Is this KazSky Adventures?"

The nearest man, stocky with a permanent scowl, crossed his arms. "You're in the wrong place. Leave. Now."

Tae stumbled dramatically, nearly losing his balance. "This is such a nice plane," he muttered, slurring his words. "Mind if I..." His sentence trailed off as he swayed again, looking ready to collapse.

Then, without warning, the clumsy act vanished. Tae straightened, his movements replaced by a cold, predatory focus. "...tear it apart?"

Before anyone could react, Tae's fist connected with the stocky man's jaw, sending him sprawling.

Derrick blinked, caught off guard by the sudden shift, but his instincts kicked in as the second man charged. He sidestepped, tripping him and shoving him toward Tae, who ended it with a swift elbow to the temple.

The third man proved quicker. His kick caught Derrick hard in the knee, sending him to the ground with a grunt of pain. Tae sighed dramatically and stepped in, locking the man in a chokehold. The guard thrashed briefly, but it was over in seconds.

As the man slumped unconscious to the floor, Tae let him drop with a thud and turned to Derrick, shaking his head. "Do I have to do everything myself?"

Derrick grimaced, rubbing his knee as he pushed himself to his feet. "Why is it always the knees?" He shot Tae a pointed look. "Next time, maybe give me a little warning before you go full John Wick?"

Tae grinned, unapologetic. "And ruin the surprise?"

After tying up the guards, Tae moved quickly through the plane, checking every compartment, locker, and hidden corner for any sign of Arabella. Derrick, meanwhile, slipped into a small office adjacent to the hangar. An old desktop computer sat on a dusty desk, humming to life as he booted it up, plugged in a drive, and started downloading every file he could access.

The room was a mess. Papers were scattered everywhere and file cabinets overflowing. As the files transferred, Derrick rummaged through drawers and folders, searching for anything that might stand out. "It worked in Nordlithia," he thought, shoving aside the frustration building with every dead end.

Minutes passed, and nothing surfaced. Invoices, maintenance logs, and mundane documents piled in his hands—nothing that connected to Arabella.

Tae stepped into the office, holding up a small object. "Found this."

Derrick moved closer to take a look. It was a delicate hairpin with a bright, playful design— something unmistakably meant for a young girl.

"You sure?" Derrick asked quietly.

Tae nodded. "The President confirmed it was hers. We're on the right trail."

Derrick exhaled heavily, running a hand through his hair. "Were. If she was here, they've already moved her—and they covered their tracks well."

Tae's gaze shifted toward the hangar, his eyes narrowing as something clicked. "Hang on," he said, already heading for the door.

Back in the hangar, the three guards lay sprawled on the ground, still unconscious. Tae grabbed a bottle of water and crouched beside one—the one who had carried himself with a little too much confidence earlier. He splashed the water over the man's face, snapping him awake.

The guard groaned, opening his eyes to Tae's icy gaze.

"Where's the girl?" Tae's voice cut through the stillness like a blade.

The guard spat something in Kazakh, his defiance clear. Tae didn't react. Instead, he reached down and yanked off the man's boot. Standing, his eyes searched the workbench nearby until they landed on a pair of pliers gleaming under the dim light. He picked them up, twirling them lazily in his hand.

The guard's confidence wavered, his eyes darting between the pliers and Tae's cold expression.

Tae crouched again, his voice calm but dripping with menace. "Let's play a game," he said, tapping the guard's big toe with the pliers. "This little piggy went to market..." He moved to the next toe. "This little piggy stayed home..."

The guard's breathing quickened, panic creeping in as Tae continued. "This little piggy had roast beef..." His tone darkened as he tapped the fourth toe. "...and this little piggy?" Tae leaned in close, his gaze locking onto the guard's wide eyes. "This little piggy is *gone*."

The pliers clamped down, and with a sharp twist, the toe snapped free. The guard's scream echoed through the hangar.

Derrick appeared in the doorway, his expression unreadable. "Tae, what are you doing?"

Tossing the severed digit aside, Tae grinned. "Shall we continue?"

Before he could press further though, a groan came from behind. One of the other guards stirred. He froze as his gaze landed on the scene—his wounded comrade writhing on the floor and Tae standing over him with cold detachment. But then his gaze shifted and a bitter chuckle escaped his lips. "I didn't know the CIA operated in Kazakhstan," he sneered.

Tae froze as the second guard's grin stretched wider. He then leaned forward as far as the restraints allowed, his eyes gleaming with satisfaction. "... Deputy Director."

The air in the hangar seemed to chill. Tae's hand hovered mid-air, his entire body tensing. For a brief moment, the guard's audacity seemed to stun him.

Derrick stepped closer, having watched the exchange. "Tae," he said, his voice a low warning.

The guard, emboldened by the flicker of hesitation, continued. "Didn't think someone at your level would get their hands this dirty. What would your boss think?"

The taunt snapped something back into place. Tae's hesitation vanished, his jaw tightening as he grabbed the guard's collar and yanked him upright. "Where's the girl?" he growled.

When the guard offered nothing but a defiant glare, Tae let out a frustrated breath. Removing a dagger from his belt, he thrust it at the man's face, stopping mere millimeters from the man's left eye.

"Last chance to *see* tomorrow."

The man gasped, his voice trembling as he blurted out, "Lake Tengiz! A compound near the shore! Please—don't—

Tae released his grip, letting the guard collapse to the ground, shaking. He stood for a moment, taking a deep breath as he processed the man's earlier words.

Derrick saw Tae's demeaner change as he crouched back down and grasp the man's head, forcing his mouth open.

Reaching in with the pliers, Tae gripped the guard's tongue, pulling it out as far as it would go.

"Thanks for the info," he said, his voice chillingly calm. "Guess you don't need this anymore. Hard to talk about me if you can't talk at all."

The guard's eyes widened in sheer terror as Tae raised the knife to his mouth and rested it on the back of his tongue.

"Tae!" Derrick's sharp voice cut through the air like a whip. "That's enough."

Tae froze, his grip still tight on the guard. Slowly, he turned his head toward Derrick, his eyes blazing with fury. Neither man moved as the tension between them crackled.

"We got what we needed," Derrick said firmly. "Let... him... go."

Tae's gaze lingered on Derrick a moment longer before he exhaled through his nose and tossed the pliers onto the ground with a metallic clang. Rising to his feet, he stared down at the trembling guard. "Next time."

The guard crumpled onto the floor, shaking and gasping for air as Derrick followed Tae out of the hangar.

Reaching Lake Tengiz by road wasn't an option—not with the distance and the clock working against them. A helicopter was their best shot, but every call Tae made hit a dead end. Local contacts, trusted resources—none of it panned out.

He ended another call as he paced near the edge of the tarmac. "Something's not right. We've attracted too much attention. Was there someone else here other than the guards?"

Derrick frowned, scrolling through his phone as he checked the security feeds they'd accessed earlier. "Could've been the guards calling for backup before we took them down—or maybe someone saw the commotion from outside the hangar."

It didn't take long for their suspicions to be confirmed. Word was spreading fast. A worker at the airfield had been overheard mentioning strangers poking around a private hangar, and within minutes, a local government official contacted Tae directly, pushing for an in-person meeting.

The tone was polite—too polite—but Derrick and Tae both recognized it for what it was: a stall tactic.

As Tae hung up, he glanced at Derrick grimly. "They're buying time."

"We need to go," Derrick said urgently, glancing at the plane.

Tae nodded. "Fallback plan—get airborne and sort it out from there."

Grabbing what they could, they bolted for the plane. The wail of sirens echoed through the air, growing louder with every step as they sprinted across the tarmac. By the time they climbed aboard, the flashing lights of police cars lit up the airport's perimeter.

The engines roared to life, and the plane taxied onto the runway, picking up speed. Derrick gripped the armrest as the aircraft hurtled forward, the vibrations rattling through his chest. Just as the wheels left the ground, a line of police cars screeched to a halt at the edge of the tarmac.

"Close call," Derrick sighed, letting out a slow breath as he sank into his seat.

Tae leaned back, rubbing a hand over his face. "Way too close." He paused, staring out the window at the shrinking airport below. "We'll regroup in Rome, but..." He shook his head, a hint of frustration creeping into his voice. "This thing's spiraling faster than I expected."

***

The plane soared through the night sky toward Rome, the adrenaline of their escape slowly giving way to an uneasy calm. Derrick sat across from Tae, who stared out the window, lost in thought.

Derrick leaned forward, arms resting on his knees. "Alright, you wanna explain what that was with the guard?" His tone carried more curiosity than judgment, but there was an edge to it.

Tae didn't turn, his focus still on the night sky. "We needed intel," he said flatly.

"Right. And the part where you *ripped off his toe*—was that necessary?" Derrick's voice rose just enough to pull Tae's attention.

He gave a slow shrug. "He wasn't using it."

"You can't just—" Derrick stopped mid-sentence, his words catching as Tae pulled something from his pocket. Without a hint of hesitation, he held up what looked like a severed finger, turning it over like he was examining a new gadget.

"This one, though? Might've been important," Tae mused, turning it in his hand as if debating its worth.

Derrick shot out of his seat, his voice echoing in the cabin. "TAE?!?!"

Tae looked up at him with a half-smile, completely unfazed. "What? He gave me the finger, so I took it." He then tucked the finger into a plastic bag with an almost nonchalant motion. "Relax. Figured you might need a spare sometime."

CHAPTER 5

The buzz of Tae's phone interrupted their conversation. A quick glance at the screen drew a sharp inhale. He muttered something under his breath before answering. "Madam Director."

The voice on the other end carried no warmth. "We've got a situation, Tae."

"What now?" Tae asked, though the sinking feeling in his chest told him he already knew the answer.

"The Kazakh government isn't just angry— they're livid. They know about the operation, and more importantly, they know you were there. They're demanding answers as to why the Deputy Director of the CIA was on their soil without approval."

Tae leaned back, rubbing his temple. "So, they didn't appreciate the surprise."

A dry, humorless chuckle followed. "That's putting it lightly. I'm doing what I can to smooth things over, but this is a mess. Your cover's blown, and they're demanding accountability. You've become too high-profile."

The pause that followed was heavy. When the Director spoke again, her tone softened slightly, though it remained firm. "You can't keep running these missions, Tae. It's over. You're coming home."

Tae sat in silence, letting the words sink in. He'd known this was coming, but hearing it still hit harder than he'd expected. His entire career had been built in the shadows, taking on dangerous, high-stakes missions. Now it was all being pulled out from under him, replaced by a desk job in DC.

Understood," he said finally, his voice flat.

"I'm sorry, Tae. We'll debrief you when you get back, but for now, lay low in Rome. Stay off the radar. This isn't just about Kazakhstan—it's going to ripple through the region."

"I'll figure it out," Tae replied, ending the call. He stared at the dark screen for a long moment before setting the phone down.

Across the aisle, Derrick let out a quiet breath and glanced his way. "That sounded bad."

Tae exhaled slowly, a faint smirk tugging at the corner of his mouth, though it didn't reach his eyes. "They're grounding me. No more missions, no more fieldwork. DC wants their shiny, new Deputy Director back where they can keep him on a leash."

Derrick leaned forward, resting his elbows on his knees. "And you? What do you want?"

"What I've always wanted," Tae muttered, his gaze shifting back to the window. "To get the job done.

To finish what we started. But looks like that's not up to me anymore."

***

Rome was quiet at this late hour. Its winding streets were nearly deserted as Derrick and Tae made their way toward the Embassy.

Inside, they spread everything they had across a conference room table. The pile wasn't much—just fragments of information and a tenuous trail—but it was all they had. Derrick paced the room, his thoughts racing as he tried to piece together their next move.

"We can't stop looking for Arabella," he said, the tension in his voice cutting through the stillness. "If we lose this trail now, she could vanish for good."

Tae nodded, though a flicker of frustration crossed his face. "I know. We're running out of options. But I might have one last card to play."

Derrick stopped pacing and turned to him. "What are you thinking?"

Pulling out his phone, Tae scrolled through his contacts. "An old friend of mine. She's good. If anyone can help you get closer, it's her."

He dialed the number, and after a few rings, a soft, confident voice answered. "Bonjour, Tae. It's been a while."

Juliette Rousseau—a seasoned Interpol agent renowned for her undercover work and connections in places most people wouldn't dare tread. She and Tae had collaborated on a few operations in the past, and while they hadn't stayed in close contact, their professional trust was unshakable.

"I'm guessing this isn't a social call."

"Not exactly," Tae admitted. "We're in a situation. My partner and I have been tracking the President's daughter. We think she was taken to Kazakhstan, but I can't continue on this. I need your help."

There was a brief pause, followed by a thoughtful hum. "Kazakhstan," she mused. "Dangerous territory."

"Believe me, I know," Tae replied. "So—are you in?"

Juliette let out a quiet laugh. "Of course. I'm already in the region. Where should I meet your partner?"

Tae glanced at Derrick. "Tashkent. Shirin's Lounge. You remember the place?"

"I do," Juliette said without hesitation. "And how will I recognize him?"

Tae smirked. "He'll be the guy who looks like he's been chasing shadows for days."

You could almost hear the smile in her reply. "Chasing shadows? Sounds promising. Tashkent it is. 1500 hours. See you soon."

The line went dead, and Tae pocketed his phone before turning to Derrick. "She's good. You can trust her. I know it's a long drive from Tashkent to the compound, but with everything going on, this is the best option. I'll handle things on this end."

Derrick let out a resigned sigh. "Tashkent."

CHAPTER 6

The airport buzzed with activity, the voices, footsteps, and announcements fading into a backdrop of muffled noise. Derrick slouched in a rigid chair near his gate, his legs stretched out in front of him, staring at the departure board without really seeing it. His flight to Tashkent wouldn't leave for another hour, and the minutes dragged by with a stubborn slowness. Commercial travel wasn't his first choice, but with Kazakhstan's borders already on edge, he had to use discretion.

Around him, families laughed, businesspeople tapped away on laptops, and vacationers flipped through magazines. Normal routines, distant from the kind of chaos Derrick carried with him. He pulled out his phone, his thumb hovering over the screen before pressing the contact he always relied on. Lydia picked up after the second ring.

"Hey," he said, shifting in his seat. The faint sound of shuffling papers and muffled conversations on her end painted a picture of the White House's constant buzz. He could picture her finding a quiet corner, trying to steal a moment of calm amidst the chaos.

"Derrick," she said, her tone warm but tinged with worry. "How are you holding up?"

"I'm managing," he replied, though they both knew it wasn't entirely true. "Still in Rome, waiting for my flight to Tashkent. I'll meet up with an Interpol contact there—someone Tae trusts. He's out, though. Cover's blown."

A brief silence filled the line, and Derrick could picture Lydia biting her lip, her usual habit when concern got the better of her. "Interpol," she said, hesitating. "Are you sure about this agent?"

Derrick tried to sound reassuring. "Tae's worked with her before. This isn't her first rodeo."

Lydia sighed softly, the sound heavy with worry she wasn't trying to hide. "I don't like you going in alone. But I know you don't have a choice. Just... don't do anything reckless. Arabella needs you. I need you."

A faint smile tugged at his lips, though the knot in his chest tightened. "I'll find her," he promised. "No matter what."

"I know you will." Lydia's voice softened, but after a pause, she shifted the subject, her attempt to ease both their nerves. "Katherine and I have been spending a lot of time together. Trying to keep her distracted, but it's hard. Madeline's been helping in her own way."

"Yeah?" Derrick asked, the tension in his shoulders easing slightly. "How's she doing?"

"Chasing Secret Service agents all over the second floor," Lydia said with a chuckle. "They're playing along, letting her 'catch' them. She's having a blast."

Derrick giggled, imagining her tormenting those poor agents. "Glad she's keeping busy. She's got them wrapped around her finger, doesn't she?"

"Completely," Lydia agreed, her tone lighter. "She misses you, though. We both do."

"I miss you too," Derrick said quietly, his grip tightening on the phone. "I'll be home soon."

For a moment, they sat in silence, letting the connection bridge the distance between them. When the overhead speaker crackled to life, announcing Derrick's flight, he exhaled and stood, grabbing his bag.

"Time to go," he said, glancing toward the gate.

"Call me when you can," Lydia said softly. "And be careful."

"I will. Love you."

"Love you too."

The call ended, leaving him standing in the middle of the bustling terminal. Sliding the phone into his pocket, he adjusted the strap on his bag and made his way toward the gate.

***

The room was dim, illuminated only by the faint glow of a desk lamp. A hand reached out, fingers curling around the corner of a folder whose edges were worn from frequent handling. The faint rustle of paper filled the silence as the folder was opened, revealing a meticulously organized dossier.

The first page bore a familiar name: *Derrick Anderson.* Beneath it, a black-and-white photo stared back, capturing a much younger him. A shadowy figure flipped to the next page, revealing detailed reports from his time at the Agency. Notations about his aptitude for strategy and marksmanship filled the margins, accompanied by redacted passages hinting at classified operations.

Further into the folder, another section emerged—this one personal. A photograph of Lydia slipped loose, accompanied by handwritten notes. It described their early relationship, her emotional connection to him, and their eventual marriage.

The pages turned again, shifting to his missions. One detailed his interactions with Obadiah in Tripoli and noting the precision with which Derrick neutralized him in North Carolina. Another chronicled Dreamweaver, outlining the procedure and code that was implanted along with the results. The section on Izzy was annotated heavily, describing her psychological warfare and Derrick's ultimate confrontation with her in the motel.

A thin document lay tucked near the back—a psychological profile. It listed his fears, triggers, and medical history. The tremors in his hands were noted in detail, as well as the scars from past events. The analysis speculated on his resilience, but the undercurrent was clear: every man had a breaking point.

"Anderson's greatest strength lies in his emotional bond with his wife, Lydia. While it fuels his determination and focus, it also presents a key vulnerability. Any threat to this bond could destabilize his otherwise unyielding resolve."

The figure paused, holding the page longer than the rest before continuing to its next section titled *"Threat Potential"*. The text beneath it was concise and chilling, written with the cold proficiency of someone assessing a weapon rather than a man.

"Anderson, Derrick: Extreme threat level. Tactical mind paired with field experience beyond standard operatives. Demonstrates an unrelenting focus under pressure and adaptive strategies even when severely compromised. Highly resistant to psychological manipulation. Known to eliminate obstacles with precision, including high-value targets and internal assets when necessary."

Further down, a subheading caught the figure's eye: *Operational History Indicators.* A bullet-point list followed:

- Neutralized Obadiah with extreme efficiency despite limited resources.
- Decimated the Dreamweaver network, countering advanced psychological operations.

- Terminated Izzy after enduring significant psychological and physical duress, showcasing critical resistance under sustained assault.

The final line on the page was stark, underscored for emphasis:

"Grave risk to operational goals. Contingency required for immediate neutralization upon intersection with primary objectives."

The figure lingered on the words, fingertips brushing over the thick paper as if weighing their implications. Slowly, the page was flipped back into place, the remaining documents tucked neatly under the folder's cover.

The dossier closed with a soft thud, but the figure didn't move. A faint vibration broke the silence, and a phone was lifted from the desk. The screen illuminated the shadowy features of the figure, but the details of their face remained obscured.

A voice crackled through the speaker as the call connected. "I got the picture you sent," the voice said smoothly. "Good job. They'll never know the difference." There was a pause, and the voice asked, "Remember the plan?"

"Of course," the figure replied before the line disconnected with a faint beep.

As they lowered the phone back to the desk, the faintest shift in the light revealed something in the background: a discarded bottle of red hair dye, its label smeared with dark stains.

They stared at the folder for a moment longer. Stamped crisply beneath *TOP SECRET\SCI* was a symbol that gleamed faintly under the dim light. The symbol belonged to Nightfall. The folder was then slid into a drawer and locked away with a soft click.

***

Derrick stepped off the plane into the dry, crisp air of Tashkent. It was mid-morning, and the sun was already climbing high. His body felt heavy, exhausted from the long flight, and sleep had evaded him. Thoughts of the mission churned in his head, gnawing at him.

The airport was bustling with the usual sights and sounds of travelers filling the air, but Derrick barely noticed. He glanced at his watch—four hours until his meeting with Juliette at Shirin's Lounge. Enough time to get his bearings and maybe pick up something for Lydia and Madeline.

He didn't know what she looked like, but he was certain she wouldn't have trouble finding him. He stood out like a sore thumb among the locals, his posture too stiff, his clothes too American. If anyone was looking for him, he'd be hard to miss.

With time to kill, Derrick walked into the streets near the airport. Rows of street vendors lined the sidewalks, selling everything from vibrant fabrics to handmade jewelry, with the sweet scent of fresh bread wafting through the air. One stall in particular caught his attention—a vendor displaying silk kurts with intricate patterns that shimmered in the sunlight.

One in particular stood out from the rest. It's deep blues and rich golds reminded him of Lydia. "She'd love something like this," he whispered to himself.

Derrick approached, and a smile tugged at his lips as he examined the craftsmanship. The vendor, an older woman with a kind, weathered face, greeted him warmly and explained the history behind the patterns in broken but enthusiastic English. Without much hesitation, Derrick purchased the dress and slid it into his pack.

Nearby, another stall displayed small, handmade toys. He couldn't help but pick up a small stuffed bear, imagining Madeline's excitement when she saw it. As he tucked the items away, a rare feeling of connection to home washed over him. In the chaos of the mission, these small gestures were a reminder of the life waiting for him, a life that felt distant and fragile.

With his purchases made, Derrick found a quiet bench beneath the shade of a tree. He sank into the seat, letting his thoughts settle. The hours would pass quickly, and soon he'd be at Shirin's Lounge, hoping Juliette was the ally he needed to bring Arabella home.

Shirin's Lounge was a quiet refuge from the noise of the city, dimly lit and cozy. The rich red walls, adorned with traditional Uzbek patterns, contrasted with the dark wood tables that seemed to hold the weight of whispered secrets. Low lamps cast an amber glow, creating a subtle, intimate atmosphere.

It was a calm spot, with only a few patrons scattered around, each wrapped in their own conversations. The stillness felt almost out of place. Derrick couldn't shake the feeling that someone was watching him as he entered. He chose a table in the back corner, one with a clear view of the entrance, and sank into the cushioned chair.

A cup of green tea arrived, the steam rising in gentle spirals, giving him something to focus on as he waited for Juliette. He had no idea what she looked like, but he trusted Tae's judgment. If anyone could help them get closer to Arabella, it was her.

CHAPTER 7

His eyes naturally scanned the room, a habit he couldn't shake, when the door opened. A woman walked in, and the room shifted. Her red hair caught the light, and her sharp green eyes swept across the space.

Derrick froze. He knew that face—it was her, from Alaska. "Cinnamon," he muttered under his breath.

Juliette moved toward him, a playful grin spreading across her face. She slid into the seat across from him like they were old friends picking up where they left off.

"Well, well, fancy seeing you again," she said with amusement. "Your wife isn't with you this time, I take it?"

Derrick blinked, still surprised by the sudden familiarity. His mind scrambled to catch up. "Almost didn't recognize you," he replied, trying to keep his surprise in check.

Juliette leaned back, casually pointing to herself with a smirk. "Oh, you mean these?" she said, indicating her chest. "Got a reduction after Kotzebue. Those things were a pain. Honestly, the worst part of that mission."

Derrick's hand went to his face. *Tae*, he thought. *I swear I'm going to kill you.*

After a few laughs about Alaska, Derrick leaned back, his tone shifting. "We need to focus. The President's daughter has been taken. I've tracked her from Nordlithia to Astana, but it's been a nightmare. Tae's out of the picture, and I need someone who can move quietly without attracting attention."

Juliette's expression faded into something more professional. "Kidnapping someone that high-profile? This isn't random. If she's still in Kazakhstan, it's not for ransom—it's leverage. Going in loud isn't an option."

"You have a better idea?" Derrick asked.

Her lips curved into a sly smile. "Of course. We go undercover. Newlyweds on a romantic adventure, exploring the beauty of Kazakhstan. Nobody bats an eye at tourists, especially happy couples on their honeymoon."

Derrick gave her a skeptical look. "Newlyweds? Really?"

"It's perfect," she insisted. "It's believable, as it gives us an excuse to travel without raising suspicion, and then we can move freely. Plus," she added with a wink, "I've always wanted to try a honeymoon in the middle of nowhere."

A pause hung between them before Derrick sighed. "Fine. Newlyweds it is."

With the plan set, they left the lounge and headed to a nearby rental agency. An hour later, they were on the road in a well-equipped SUV, stocked with supplies for the journey ahead.

The tires hummed along the open highway, the horizon stretching endlessly under the bright afternoon sun. Derrick gripped the steering wheel with both hands, his knuckles white as they approached the border checkpoint. The vast expanse of the steppe offered no cover, no backup plan. His gaze flicked between the rearview mirror and the guards ahead.

Next to him, Juliette lounged in her seat, exuding an effortless calm. "Relax," she remarked, not bothering to look over. "You're supposed to be a man madly in love. Try smiling."

"Smiling doesn't help if they decide to search the car," Derrick grumbled, his grip tightening.

As the checkpoint loomed closer, a guard in a dark uniform raised a hand, signaling them to stop. Derrick rolled the window down, forcing a polite nod while the guard scanned the vehicle.

"Papers," the guard barked in Kazakh, his tone curt.

Juliette leaned over, flashing a flirtatious smile as she handed over the documents. "Of course," she said in fluid Kazakh, her voice warm and casual. "We're on our honeymoon, just driving through to see your beautiful country."

The guard's eyes narrowed as he examined the papers. Another guard joined him, both peering into the car. Derrick kept his expression neutral, letting Juliette handle the moment.

She didn't falter. Leaning her elbow on the doorframe, she began chatting with the guards, her tone friendly and light. Compliments about the region, a laugh here and there—her charm was effortless. Derrick stayed silent, trying not to look like someone sneaking into hostile territory.

Seconds stretched into what felt like hours before the guards exchanged a glance. One of them handed the papers back, his demeanor softening. "Enjoy your trip," he said, stepping away and waving them through.

Juliette shot the guard a wink. "Thanks, honey."

As they drove past the checkpoint, Derrick exhaled slowly, releasing the tension in his shoulders. "That was way too close."

Juliette chuckled, her gaze still on the road ahead. "You looked like you were smuggling dead bodies in the trunk."

"I'm not exactly cut out for undercover as a honeymooner," he groaned, shaking his head.

"Good thing you've got me," she quipped, a teasing grin on her lips. "You'd be terrible at this without me."

The road stretched endlessly ahead, barren and unchanging. Dusty hues of brown and green blurred together as hours passed, the isolation of the Kazakh steppe settling in. Villages were rare out here, just scattered clusters of weathered buildings that seemed to defy the emptiness around them. As the sun dipped closer to the horizon, they spotted a modest town, its few lights flickering to life.

Juliette leaned forward, studying the small inn near the center of the town. "Looks like our best bet," she said, her voice breaking the silence. "Unless you're up for sleeping in the car."

Derrick shook his head, steering into the inn's dirt lot. "I've had better ideas."

The inn was simple, its exterior worn but inviting. Inside, the dining area was just as unassuming—wooden tables and chairs scattered across the room, the scent of freshly baked bread hanging in the air. A quiet corner near the back seemed like the safest place to settle without attracting attention.

Dinner arrived quickly: hearty portions of seasoned meat, rice, and flatbread. Derrick picked at his food, his thoughts far from the table. The mission loomed large in his mind, every unanswered question gnawing at him. Across from him, Juliette ate with ease, her relaxed demeanor almost infuriating.

"You're thinking too much," she said, not looking up from her plate. "You'll burn out before we even get there."

"It's hard not to," Derrick admitted. "Every second we waste, she's—"

Juliette's sharp look cut him off. "And you won't help her by spiraling into a mess of 'what ifs.' Eat. Sleep. Focus when it matters."

For a moment, he said nothing, then finally picked up his fork again. She wasn't wrong, though he wasn't about to admit it.

The innkeeper handed over the key with a warm smile, gesturing toward the narrow staircase that led to the rooms. Derrick glanced down at the single key in his hand, his chest tightening as he understood what it meant.

Juliette, ever composed, breezed past him and started up the stairs. "Coming?" she asked over her shoulder, as if this arrangement was entirely normal.

The room was small but clean. Faded floral curtains framed a single window, and a queen-sized bed dominated the space. Derrick stood in the doorway, feeling like the walls were already closing in.

Juliette tossed her bag onto the bed and unzipped it without a second glance. "This'll do," she said, rifling through her belongings.

"There's only one bed," Derrick pointed out, his voice a little sharper than intended.

Her gaze flicked to the bed, then back to him. "Observant," she said sarcastically.

"I'll take the chair," Derrick said, dragging it noisily from the corner of the room and planting it next to the bed. He sat down with a huff, feet propped on the mattress.

Juliette vanished into the bathroom without another word. When she reappeared, her hair was tied back, and she'd swapped her travel clothes for a tank top and shorts. She stretched lazily, ignoring Derrick's pointed effort to look anywhere but at her.

"This is for Arabella," he muttered under his breath. "For Arabella."

The corner of Juliette's mouth quirked upward as she slid under the covers. "Talking to yourself already? I hope I'm not that intimidating."

Derrick scowled, shifting in his chair. "I just want to get this over with."

"Relax, Romeo," she said, rolling onto her side. "I'm not going to bite. Unless you snore, then all bets are off."

Groaning, Derrick leaned his head back against the chair. Sleep already felt like a distant dream.

"You know," she said after a moment, "we could share. The bed's big enough."

He sat up straighter, eyes narrowing. "I'm married. You met Lydia."

Juliette raised a hand, feigning innocence. "Calm down. I'm just saying you'll wake up with a crick in your neck if you stay in that chair. Lydia would probably agree."

"Not happening," Derrick said firmly, arms crossed.

"Suit yourself." She rolled onto her back, a soft laugh escaping. "I'd hate to see how awkward you were on your real honeymoon."

Another groan escaped him as he leaned back, closing his eyes. It was going to be a very long night.

***

A stiff neck and aching back greeted Derrick as he stirred awake. Hours in the unforgiving chair had left his muscles protesting, each movement a reminder of his stubborn decision to avoid the bed. The temptation to slide under the covers beside Juliette had crept in more than once during the night, but his thoughts had drifted instead to Lydia—the life they shared, the family waiting for him. That love was unshakable. While Derrick knew he wouldn't do anything, just the presence of the temptation was enough to keep him securely in his chair.

Stretching to work out the knots in his back, he caught a subtle scent in the air—strawberries. The same perfume Lydia wore. For a fleeting moment, his thoughts wavered, pulling him back to warm mornings and her laughter filling their home. The memory faded as he rubbed the ache from his neck, grounding himself in the present.

Juliette, already dressed and fresh-faced, zipped her bag closed. A playful smile tugged at her lips as she slung the strap over her shoulder. "Rough night?"

"The chair," Derrick muttered, shooting it a look of disdain. "Never again."

Her laugh was soft, laced with just enough teasing to make his shoulders relax despite the soreness. "Could've joined me, you know. The bed's not cursed."

Pulling on his jacket, Derrick shook his head, ignoring the comment. "Let's just get moving."

"Suit yourself, Romeo," she said, the grin widening. "Breakfast awaits."

Downstairs, the inn's small dining area was quiet, the early morning light streaming through the windows. They grabbed a simple breakfast—eggs, bread, and strong coffee—before spreading out their map to plan the day's route. Eight hours on remote roads lay ahead, and neither seemed eager to linger.

The SUV roared to life, and they hit the road with the early sun stretching over the wilderness. Rolling hills and open grasslands unfolded around them, the desolation broken only by the occasional flock of sheep or rusted roadside sign. For the first few hours, the silence stretched comfortably between them as they focused on the road ahead.

Eventually, the quiet gave way to conversation. Derrick talked about his childhood in Texas, the relentless curiosity that had propelled him to MIT, and the unexpected path that led him to the CIA. Juliette's story, in turn, unraveled like a tapestry—her adventurous youth in the south of France, the fearless curiosity that had drawn her to Interpol, and the dangerous dance of undercover missions that had become her life.

Her stories had a vividness that pulled Derrick in, painting a picture of someone who thrived on the thrill of the unknown. Beneath her composed exterior, he caught glimpses of vulnerability, moments she seemed to share without realizing.

"You've seen more than most people ever will," Derrick remarked. "Does it ever... get to you?"

Juliette's hand brushed a loose strand of hair from her face as she considered the question. "Sometimes," she admitted. "But it's part of the job. You find ways to carry it, to let it shape you without breaking you." Her green eyes flicked to him briefly, gauging his reaction. "You'd know all about that though, wouldn't you?"

A quiet smile curved his lips. "More than I'd like."

The conversation drifted to lighter topics, old missions filled with missteps and close calls. Juliette's laugh came easily now, her teasing keeping the mood light. Derrick found himself chuckling more than he expected as the miles slipped by into the distance.

"You're an odd one, Derrick," she said finally, her tone light but sincere. "Interesting, though."

He raised an eyebrow, glancing at her with a faint smirk. "Interesting? That's one way to put it."

Juliette's smile lingered, her gaze fixed on the road ahead. "It's a compliment. I don't give them out often."

***

Tae walked briskly down the hall of the White House, his thoughts already on his upcoming meeting with President Green. As he passed one of the sitting rooms, he spotted Lydia deep in conversation with Katherine. She looked up, met his eyes, and offered a smile before excusing herself.

"Tae," she said warmly, pulling him into a quick hug. "Any word on Derrick?"

"They're headed to the compound," Tae replied. "He met up with the Interpol contact I arranged—Juliette."

Her curiosity was immediate, her expression shifting as she tilted her head slightly. "Juliette?"

"That's right," Tae said, nodding. "Tough, resourceful. You've actually met her before."

Lydia frowned, sifting through her memory. "I have? I don't recognize the name."

The grin spreading across Tae's face hinted at the punchline coming. "You might know her better as... Cinnamon."

Her eyes widened in disbelief. "The stripper?!"

"She was undercover," he said, holding back a laugh. "Mission work."

Lydia stared at him for a moment, then burst into laughter, shaking her head. "Well, she certainly made an impression on Derrick."

CHAPTER 8

As the last traces of sunlight faded, Derrick and Juliette crouched near the edge of the facility. The barren expanse around them felt even more desolate in the growing darkness, with only the faint hum of wind breaking the silence. Ahead, the compound sprawled, its central building surrounded by dimly lit outposts and the occasional patrol.

Through her binoculars, Juliette studied the layout. "That one," she murmured, nodding toward the three-story structure in the middle. "Looks like the main target. Security's tighter there."

Derrick's gaze followed hers. The building stood apart, more fortified than the others. "We wait until it's completely dark."

When night fully settled, the compound seemed to sink into an eerie silence. Juliette led the way, slipping through the gaps between buildings. Derrick kept close, sweeping the area for any signs of trouble. At the rear of the central building, they paused. Derrick crouched by the door, tools in hand. After a few tense seconds, the lock gave way with a soft click.

Inside, the air felt heavy and was eerily quiet. The dim lighting barely illuminated the narrow halls.

Room by room, they searched the first and second floors, but they held nothing but hastily emptied rooms and faint signs of recent activity.

"Nothing," Juliette muttered, frustration creeping into her voice.

"There has to be something here," Derrick replied, his gut refusing to let him believe otherwise.

At the base of the stairs to the third floor, they froze. Footsteps echoed faintly above, growing louder with each passing second. Juliette drew her weapon as Derrick gestured for silence. With Juliette leading, they crept up the stairs, staying close to the wall. Just as they reached the landing, gunfire shattered the stillness, a sharp burst of gunshots sending them diving for cover.

"Down!" Juliette hissed, firing back at the group of armed men at the end of the corridor.

Derrick cursed under his breath. Commercial travel had left him unarmed, and the odds weren't in their favor. Scanning the room nearest him, he spotted a cabinet under the sink. Inside, a mix of cleaning supplies and basic tools caught his eye. A plan formed.

Grabbing a bottle of drain cleaner, aluminum foil, and the small trash can, he worked quickly. The chemicals hissed and bubbled as he dropped crumpled balls of foil into the can.

"Juliette, cover!" he shouted, shoving the makeshift device into the hallway.

She ducked without hesitation, pressing herself against the wall as thick, acrid smoke erupted, filling the corridor in seconds. The gunfire ceased, replaced by coughing and the sound of retreating footsteps.

When the smoke thinned, Derrick and Juliette advanced cautiously, finding the hallway was now empty.

"They pulled back," she said, scanning the area in frustration.

At the far end of the corridor, a partially open door caught their attention. Inside, the room was stark—just a small bed with crumpled blankets and a few scattered toys. Juliette knelt, examining the space.

"She was here," she said quietly, holding up a child's stuffed animal.

From the window, Derrick spotted movement in the distance. Two trucks barreled down a dirt road, their taillights cutting through the night. "They've got her," he said, pointing toward the vehicles.

Juliette yelled something in French that would have made even French sailors take notice.

Pulling out his phone, Derrick dialed Tae. The call connected after a few rings. She was here, Tae," he said, his voice breathless as they sprinted back down the stairs. "Two trucks just left the compound. We need eyes on them."

"I'm pulling satellite feeds now," Tae replied. The sound of rapid typing filled the line. "Hang on."

Reaching their vehicle, Derrick started the engine as Juliette climbed in. The tires kicked up gravel as they sped away from the compound, the dirt road stretching into the night.

"I've got them," Tae said after a brief pause. "But they split up—one's heading north, the other south."

Derrick clenched his jaw. "We'll take the southern route. Track the northern one and update me."

"On it!" Tae said. "I'll keep you updated."

Gripping the wheel tightly, Derrick fixed his focus ahead, pushing the SUV to go faster. The chase was on.

The drive was anything but smooth. Each sharp curve appeared without warning, forcing Derrick to yank the wheel to keep the SUV from sliding off into the dark abyss beyond. Loose gravel spit from under the tires, and his grip on the wheel tightened with each near-miss.

"I hate this place," Derrick growled, jaw clenched as he forced the vehicle back on track.

"Just don't lose it now," Juliette said, her eyes fixed ahead. "We're close."

After what felt like an eternity, they finally caught sight of the truck in the small town of

Zhanbobek. It had stopped at a gas station to fill up. Derrick pulled the SUV to a halt a safe distance away.

Without hesitation, he unbuckled and reached for the door. "Stay here. I'll take a look."

Juliette smirked. "Don't get yourself killed."

Sliding into the darkness, Derrick kept low as he approached the truck. When he reached the back, he carefully pulled open the rear door. Inside, instead of Arabella, he found three armed operatives. One of them turned toward the sound, his eyes narrowing.

"Well... hello there," Derrick said, just as surprised as they were. He yanked the door wide and grabbed the edge of a heavy tool case inside, hurling it toward the nearest operative. It caught the man in the chest, knocking him backward into his comrade.

The third operative scrambled for his weapon, but Derrick was already moving. He ducked under the barrel of the rifle, slamming his shoulder into the man's midsection. Using the confined space to his advantage, Derrick shoved the operative against the side of the truck and twisted the weapon from his hands.

The first man recovered, lunging with a knife. Derrick spun, deflecting the attack with the rifle and sending the blade clattering to the floor. Before the he could regroup, Derrick drove the butt of the rifle into the man's knee, dropping him to the ground with a grunt.

The second operative, finally untangled, came at Derrick from the side. He managed to grab Derrick's arm, but he used the grip against him, spinning into the motion and slamming the operative's head against the truck's metal frame. The man slumped, dazed.

Juliette rounded the corner just as Derrick twisted the knife-wielder into a headlock, cutting off the fight with a sharp takedown.

She surveyed the scene, her eyebrows arching as she stepped closer. "Having fun without me?"

Derrick crouched, catching his breath as he grabbed a rifle from the floor and checked it quickly. "Handled it," he nonchalantly replied, "but Arabella's not here."

"Figures," she said, scanning the truck's interior. "At least you're armed now. Let's move. We still have another lead."

CHAPTER 9

The SUV hummed along the empty road, the tires eating up the miles toward Kostanay. Derrick slumped against the seat, his head tilted back and his eyes half-closed. Exhaustion weighed on him, but sleep wouldn't come. His mind churned through possibilities, running and rerunning the same scenarios like a broken record.

The silence was broken by the chime of Derrick's phone. Tae's name flashed on the screen.

"Talk to me," Derrick said, answering immediately.

"Got a brief window," Tae replied. "The truck paused in Kostanay, downtown area. No new sightings yet—too much interference from the buildings—but it's gotta be close. I'll keep digging."

Derrick pinched the bridge of his nose. "How far are we?"

"Another few hours at least," Juliette said, overhearing.

"We'll check in when we get there," Derrick said to Tae, ending the call and letting the phone drop into his lap.

By the time they reached Kostanay, it was well into the next afternoon. The noise, the movement, and the sheer density of people felt overwhelming after the solitude of the drive. Derrick's nerves frayed further with every honk and shouted conversation.

Juliette weaved through traffic as she navigated toward their destination. "First stop is the hotel," she said, not giving him room to argue. "You look like you're about to keel over."

Derrick leaned his head against the window, the cool glass a fleeting relief. "I'm fine," he sighed, though his voice lacked conviction.

Juliette gave him a quick look, her eyes narrowing slightly. "You're clutching your head like it's about to explode. Are you sure you're okay?"

"It's just a headache," he replied, massaging his temple with his free hand. "I've had worse."

She didn't look convinced but chose not to press further. He didn't bother protesting about the hotel stop either. His mind was too fogged to argue, let alone plan.

She parked outside the Medeu Hotel, a modest building nestled in a quieter part of the city. The white facade and neatly trimmed shrubs gave it a sense of calm Derrick desperately needed. Inside, the lobby's cool air and soft murmurs from the front desk felt worlds away from the chaos outside.

After checking in, they took the elevator to their room. Derrick opened the door, feeling a flicker of relief when he saw two twin beds instead of one.

"Thank God," he mumbled, toeing off his shoes before collapsing onto the bed nearest the window.

Juliette leaned against the doorframe, watching him with an amused look. "You're welcome. I made sure they had separate beds. Figured you'd want to avoid another awkward chair situation."

Derrick gave a noncommittal grunt, already half-asleep. The last thing he heard before drifting off was Juliette's quiet chuckle as she closed the door.

***

The next morning, Derrick woke to a dull ache on his forehead. He blinked groggily, his senses slowly returning as he became aware of someone touching him, the faint scent of strawberries teasing his senses.

When his eyes focused, he saw Juliette sitting beside him, carefully applying ointment to a cut he hadn't even realized he had.

"It's just me," she said softly, her voice reassuring as she continued her work. The ointment stung slightly as she dabbed at the wound.

Derrick exhaled, the tension easing from his body. "How bad is it?" he rasped, his voice rough from sleep.

"Not bad," Juliette replied lightly. "You must've hit it during the fight yesterday."

Derrick chuckled dryly. "Yeah… pretty sure I hit it on his fist."

Her smirk widened, though she stayed focused on her task. Derrick watched her silently, his fatigue leaving him too tired to protest. The quiet care she showed unsettled him—not because it was unwelcome, but because it felt too natural.

She finished and leaned back slightly, meeting his gaze. For a fleeting moment, there was an unspoken charge in the room, something just out of reach. Her expression softened, but she didn't say anything. Instead, she leaned in, brushing a quick, almost teasing kiss over the cut on his forehead.

He froze, not sure what to make of it. Her move was so casual, so matter-of-fact, that by the time he processed it, she was already grabbing her bag and heading for the door.

"Get ready," she said over her shoulder, her tone light but with that familiar edge of command. "We've got work to do."

Derrick sat there for a moment longer, processing. Finally, he shook his head, muttering under his breath, "Arabella. Focus, Derrick." With a sigh, he pushed the moment aside and began to get ready.

Derrick and Juliette made their way to the location where the satellite had lost track of the truck. Kostanay's downtown surprised him—a bustling, modern hub with sleek buildings, bright signage, and throngs of people. It was a stark contrast to the barren roads they had driven to get here.

Derrick scanned the streets, his focus narrowing on the task ahead. Somewhere in this maze, the truck had disappeared, and he wasn't leaving without answers.

"We'll need to ask around. Shops, street vendors, anyone who might've noticed a truck like the one we're tracking."

"Sounds like a plan," Derrick said, bracing himself for hours of legwork.

They spent the day weaving through streets and knocking on doors asking questions. Despite their persistence, no one had useful information. The truck had vanished, seemingly swallowed by the city. By the time the sun began to set, frustration started to gnaw at them.

"We're not getting anywhere," Juliette admitted with a sigh, brushing a strand of hair from her face. "Let's regroup. We'll have dinner, go over the maps again, and see if we missed something."

Derrick agreed.

Returning to the hotel, Derrick leaned his head against the cool glass of the passenger window, his mind replaying every missed lead and dead trail. Juliette remained focused on the road, her fingers lightly tapping the wheel, the only indication of her own frayed patience.

Once inside their room, Juliette grabbed her bag and headed straight for the shower, leaving Derrick to sink onto the edge of his bed. He kicked off his boots and rubbed his temples, willing himself to find the energy to stay awake.

He pulled out his phone and texted Lydia.

"Hey. We're back at the hotel. Heading to dinner soon."

Lydia's reply came almost instantly:

"Glad to hear you're okay. How's it going? You holding up?"

Derrick let out a long breath. He didn't want to tell Lydia the truth. He was exhausted, but wanted to sound strong for her.

"We searched all day, but turned up nothing. We'll find her though."

There was just enough of a pause to let Derrick nod off for a moment before his phone vibrated again.

"Please take care of yourself. I miss you. So does Madeline."

Derrick replied, *"I will. I miss you both too."*

When Juliette emerged, she was wrapped in a towel, her damp hair falling in loose waves around her shoulders. "Shower's all yours," she said lightly, tossing her toiletries onto the desk.

Derrick stood and stretched, his muscles stiff from the day's exertion. The hot water did little to ease the ache in his shoulders as he stood under the spray, letting the exhaustion seep out of him. After washing up, he dried off and lingered in front of the mirror.

The man staring back at him looked foreign. Dark bags under his eyes and stubble creeping along his jaw made him look older than he felt. His shoulders sagged slightly, his posture betraying the weariness he carried. He knew he couldn't stop now—Arabella's life depended on him—but the toll of the mission was undeniable.

He dressed slowly, pulling on a clean shirt and dark slacks. As he stepped out of the bathroom, he froze mid-step.

Juliette was sitting on the edge of the bed, strapping on her heels. The maroon sequin dress she wore shimmered under the dim light, hugging her frame with effortless elegance. For a moment, Derrick was taken aback—not just by how stunning she looked, but by how familiar it felt. The dress was uncannily similar to the one Lydia had worn in Monaco years ago. The memory hit him like a jolt, his mind flashing to the way Lydia had smiled at him that night, how she'd reached for his hand as they strolled through the warm evening air.

"You clean up nice," Juliette said with a smile, breaking the silence.

Derrick blinked, clearing his throat as he pulled on his jacket. "You too. That's... quite a dress."

"Figured I'd try to bring a little class to this operation," she teased, standing and smoothing the fabric.

Juliette had chosen *Arlanskaya*, a restaurant known for its intimate atmosphere. Derrick wasn't prepared for the soft candlelight that bathed the room in a warm, romantic glow. The quiet hum of conversation and the clinking of silverware added to the subdued ambiance, making it feel worlds away from the mission they were on.

Seated across from her, Derrick felt himself relax more than he expected. The day's frustrations faded slightly as the conversation turned from logistics to something lighter.

Juliette spoke first, recounting her childhood in the south of France. Her voice carried a warmth he hadn't noticed before as she shared stories of mischief and adventure, painting vivid pictures of seaside towns and bustling markets. Derrick found himself laughing at her tale of sneaking into a vineyard as a teenager, only to be caught and made to help harvest grapes as punishment.

"You're surprisingly bad at getting away with things," Derrick said with a smirk, his arms crossed as he leaned back in his chair.

"Oh, I got better," Juliette replied with a sly grin. "You don't survive in our line of work by staying predictable."

The mood lightened further as Derrick shared pieces of his own past—growing up in the Midwest, the time he and a friend rigged a sprinkler to spray unsuspecting neighbors, and even a few other childhood pranks he hadn't thought about in years. Juliette listened intently, her emerald eyes locked on him in a way that made him feel oddly at ease.

But then the realization struck.

He wasn't just talking to Juliette. He was sharing things, laughing, engaging in a way that felt too familiar—like the way he talked with Lydia on their quiet evenings at home. The realization hit hard, and guilt twisted in his chest.

"Excuse me," Derrick said abruptly, standing and heading toward the restroom.

Cold water splashed onto his face as he gripped the edges of the sink. His breathing was steady, but his mind raced. This wasn't right. Juliette wasn't Lydia, and no amount of shared laughs or easy conversation could change that.

"Focus," he muttered to himself, staring at his reflection. "Arabella. That's all that matters."

Juliette's gaze lingered as Derrick returned to the table, softer than before, leaving him uneasy. He averted his eyes, focusing on his napkin as he sat down. Before either of them could say anything, the waiter appeared with the check, breaking the silence. Derrick reached for his wallet, but Juliette waved him off.

"I've got this," she said with a faint smile. "Consider it a thank-you for the entertainment."

He nodded, not arguing, and they left the restaurant in near silence. The drive back to the hotel felt even quieter, the tension from earlier hanging in the air. Derrick kept his eyes on the road ahead, grateful Juliette seemed content not to press him further.

Back in their room, Juliette grabbed her bag and headed to the bathroom without a word. Derrick let out a breath, moving to the other side of the room to change. Exhaustion tugged at him, but his mind refused to shut off. Pulling on a fresh shirt, he sat on the edge of the bed, phone in hand, and typed out a quick message to Lydia:

"Back at the hotel, getting ready for bed. Love you."

The reply came almost instantly—a photo of Lydia and Madeline, both smiling brightly. Madeline held up a drawing, the lines crooked but unmistakably meant to be Derrick in his CIA suit.

A tear crept down his face as he stared at the picture, his thumb brushing over the screen. They looked so happy, so far removed from the chaos he was entrenched in. For a moment, the image brought a sense of calm, grounding him in a way nothing else could.

The bathroom door opened, and Juliette stepped out. Her flowing hair framed her face as she crossed the room in shorts and a tank top. Derrick shoved his phone into his pocket, standing abruptly as if caught in the middle of something.

Juliette tilted her head, her expression curious. "You're awful jumpy tonight," she said, a trace of amusement in her voice. "Something on your mind?"

"I'm fine," he replied quickly, the words coming out too sharp. "Just thinking about Arabella."

Her gaze lingered for a second longer, before she gave him a half-smile. "Arabella, huh? Sure it's not you feeling guilty that we're sharing a room?"

Derrick blinked, caught off guard. "What's that supposed to mean?"

"I just wonder what your *wifeypoo* would think of you bunking with me," she teased, though her eyes held a glimmer of curiosity.

Derrick looked somewhat confused at her. "She understands. Lydia trusts me."

The simple response hit harder than Juliette expected. She'd asked the question to poke at him, maybe throw him off balance, but his answer was too confident—no hesitation, no defensiveness. It stirred something she didn't like to acknowledge, a thought she quickly shoved aside.

"Well," she said with a playful shrug, covering the shift in her mood, "I hope I live up to her *high* standards."

He smirked faintly, brushing past her comment. "Goodnight, Juliette."

"Bonsoir, Derrick," she replied, the humor still in her tone, but her mind lingered on his words. *She trusts him?*

Without another word, Derrick slid under the covers and turned his back to her, pulling his phone out again. Lydia's message still glowed on the screen. He stared at it once more, letting their smiles ease the tension gripping him.

"I miss you both," he typed back, his fingers hovering over the send button before finally pressing it.

The room fell silent except for the faint rustle of pages as Juliette flipped through her book. Slowly, the images of Lydia and Madeline in his mind dulled the chaos swirling in his thoughts. The exhaustion won, pulling him under within moments.

Sleep came, but peace didn't follow. Derrick's mind plunged into a nightmare so vivid it consumed him entirely.

...He stood in a dark, featureless room, the only light coming from a massive screen flickering to life in front of him. Two separate chambers appeared on the screen. In one, Juliette held Arabella tightly, her

expression taut with fear. In the other, Lydia stood protectively over Madeline, her arms wrapped firmly around their daughter.

A voice thundered overhead. "You can only save one, Derrick. Make your choice."

The air in his lungs froze. His heart pounded as he stared at the screen, his mind screaming for a way out. There was no choice—it wasn't even a question. "Lydia," he rasped, his voice shaking. It was always Lydia. Always her and Madeline.

The voice returned, icy and mocking. "Wrong choice."

Derrick's blood turned to ice as the scene on the screen began to shift. An executioner stepped into the chamber with Lydia and Madeline, his face obscured by a dark hood, a gleaming blade in his hand. Derrick's legs buckled as he tried to move, to scream, to do anything, but his body refused to obey. He was frozen in place, a helpless witness.

"No!" The word tore from his throat, raw and broken, as he watched the executioner advance. Lydia's eyes locked onto the camera, wide with terror, while Madeline buried her face in her mother's chest, her small shoulders trembling.

"Don't do this!" he begged, his voice cracking. "Please!"

The screen flickered as the executioner raised the blade. A deafening silence engulfed the room. The moment stretched into eternity, the air heavy with inevitability. The blade began to fall...

Derrick shot upright in bed, a scream ripping from his throat. His chest heaved as if he were drowning, every breath shallow and frantic. Sweat dripped from his face, soaking the sheets beneath him.

Juliette was by his side in an instant. "Derrick!" she exclaimed, reaching for him. "You're okay. You're safe."

The words barely registered. The nightmare's grip still held tight, suffocating him. His breaths came in shallow, frantic gasps as panic clawed at his chest.

Juliette pulled him into her arms, holding him tightly. "Shh, breathe. Just breathe," she whispered, rocking him gently.

Derrick buried his face in her chest, his heart hammering as he tried to steady himself. Slowly, her words broke through the haze. His breaths steadied, each one deeper than the last. His trembling began to ease as he focused on her words. Gradually, the panic ebbed, leaving him drained but more in control. He pulled back slightly, his hands still shaking.

"I'm okay," he said, his voice barely more than a whisper, though he wasn't sure if he was trying to convince her or himself.

Juliette loosened her hold but didn't pull away completely. "You scared the daylights out of me," she said quietly, her voice laced with genuine worry. "What happened?"

His jaw tightened. The images still clung to him, vivid and cruel. "Just a nightmare," he said quietly, his tone clipped, as if saying it aloud would strip it of its power.

She didn't press him, her hand lingering briefly on his arm before she shifted back. "Well," she said gently, her voice softer now, "you're not alone, Derrick. Remember that."

***

Derrick woke with his muscles still tense, the remnants of the nightmare refusing to fade. His heart hadn't fully settled, and the memory of Lydia and Juliette in those impossible chambers played on a loop in his mind. A choice. That's what the voice demanded, but the dream felt heavier than that—like something more than his subconscious at work.

The room was quiet, the only sound was the window air conditioning rattling. Juliette stirred on her side of the room, stretching before sliding out of bed. She glanced at him briefly, her tone light as she said, "I'm going to grab us some coffee." Without waiting for a response, she left, the door clicking softly behind her.

Derrick sat up slowly, dragging a hand down his face before heading to the bathroom. Hot water poured over him, easing the knots in his shoulders. He leaned his head against the cool tile, eyes closed, hoping to drown the echoes of his dream in the steady rhythm of the shower.

Lydia.

Her name was a constant, the only thing steady in his racing thoughts. He could see her clearly—the softness of her smile, the warmth in her eyes, the way she could ground him with just a few words. She always seemed to know how to cut through his doubt, her voice steadying him when everything else spun out of control.

He exhaled deeply, running a hand through his hair. The mission felt heavier without her, though he was grateful she and Madeline were safe, far from the chaos he faced here. But that comfort didn't quiet the gnawing guilt, the thorn in his chest that came from memories of the night before—of Juliette's steady arms around him, the warmth of her voice breaking through his panic.

Stepping out of the shower, Derrick dried off and began to dress, his movements mechanical. Buttoning his shirt, he heard the soft click of the door. Juliette walked in, balancing two steaming cups of coffee.

"Morning," she said brightly, her smile warm enough to brighten the dim room. She placed one of the cups on the small table near his bed. "You still clean up nice," she teased, her tone playful.

Derrick offered a small grin, though it didn't quite reach his eyes. "Thanks," he said, taking the coffee and sitting on the edge of the bed.

Her gaze lingered, the easy banter giving way to something more serious. "You okay?" she asked, tilting her head slightly.

"Yeah," he said quickly, grabbing the coffee and taking a sip. The words came too fast, and he knew she caught it.

She didn't press, though the look she gave him felt almost too perceptive. "Well, caffeine works wonders. We've got a long day ahead, and I don't think either of us can handle it without some fuel."

The morning had been a series of dead ends. Warehouse after warehouse revealed nothing more than dust-covered crates and forgotten machinery. But as they approached the next target on the outskirts of town, Derrick felt the familiar prickle of unease. This one was different.

A tall, reinforced fence encircled the property, and armed guards patrolled the perimeter with a vigilance that didn't match a typical storage facility.

"Real subtle," Derrick stated, his tone dry as he surveyed the scene.

Juliette smirked. "Definitely not storing potatoes."

They parked the SUV at a safe distance, slipping out quietly. Derrick led them along the fence line until they found a weak point. Pulling wire cutters from his bag, he worked quickly, cutting just enough to create an entry point. They crouched low and slipped through, sticking to the cover of the trees and brush as they approached the warehouse.

Once they were near the building, they found a door and made their way inside, careful not to alert the guards. The interior was massive, with rows of towering crates and industrial equipment.

The air was heavy with the scent of oil and metal. Derrick's eyes darted between the rows, his senses on high alert. Ahead, a metal staircase spiraled up to a glass-walled office overlooking the warehouse floor. Juliette signaled for them to move. The stairs creaked faintly under their weight as they ascended, but no alarm sounded.

At the top, Derrick peered through the glass. Relief and dread collided in his chest.

Arabella.

She sat on a cot in the corner of the room with her knees pulled up to her chest. Though she looked tired, she didn't appear hurt.

"We've got her," Derrick whispered, relief washing over him.

But the relief was short-lived. Movement on the floor below caught his eye—a guard, too close to their position. The man froze for a second, then barked an alarm into his radio. Sirens wailed, red lights flashing in a chaotic rhythm. The room erupted into chaos. Guards burst into the office, grabbing Arabella and dragging her out the back door. Derrick's chest tightened as he watched her disappear, helpless to intervene. Gunfire crackled from below, a sharp sting tearing through his arm as he ducked behind a crate. Blood seeped through his sleeve, but he ignored it, his focus locked on Juliette as she returned fire.

"They're moving her!" Juliette shouted, her voice rising over the clamor.

Outside, the rumble of engines cut through the chaos. Trucks roared to life, their tires spinning as they sped toward the main gate.

Derrick and Juliette barely made it out of the building, weaving through the maze of crates and dodging bursts of gunfire. The guards' shots peppered the ground around them as they dove into the brush, scrambling toward the fence. Derrick winced, clutching his arm as they slipped through the cut in the chain link and sprinted for the SUV.

Juliette slammed the vehicle into gear, dirt and gravel spraying as they tore down the road. Derrick pulled his phone from his pocket with shaking hands, dialing Tae.

"They've got her," he said, breathless. "We saw her. They're moving her now—two trucks, headed north. Can you track them?"

Tae's voice was calm. "I'll get eyes on them. Stand by. And Derrick? Don't get dead."

Back at the hotel, the adrenaline had faded, leaving Derrick acutely aware of the throbbing pain in his arm. Once inside their room, Juliette wasted no time retrieving the first-aid kit.

"Sit," she instructed, her tone sympathetic.

Derrick resisted at first. "We don't have time. Tae is tracking her into Russia. We gotta move."

Juliette was unamused. "You know as well as I, we need visas to get into Russia. Tae said he was working on them. Now sit!"

Derrick dropped into the chair by the window, leaning back as she crouched beside him. The antiseptic stung as she cleaned the graze, but he didn't flinch.

"You'll live," she said, a faint smirk playing on her lips.

As she worked, tension crept into the atmosphere of the room. Juliette lingered a moment longer than necessary, her fingers lightly brushing against his arm.

Derrick's jaw tightened. The shift in her demeanor wasn't overt, but it was enough to put him on edge. Juliette's sharp professionalism had softened, replaced by something harder to ignore.

"Thanks," he said, keeping his tone neutral as he pulled his arm back.

"We should hear from Tae soon," Juliette said as she stood up. Her voice was more professional again, but the softness still lingered. "Once the visas come through, we'll head straight to Russia."

Derrick nodded, feeling the awkwardness settle between them like an invisible wall.

Juliette sighed, crossing to her bed. "Get some rest while we can. Something tells me the next leg of this trip won't leave much time for sleeping."

Hours passed in silence, broken only by the occasional notification tone from their phones. The tension between them from earlier had eased as they both settled into the waiting game.

Eventually, Derrick spoke, his voice softer than before. "Do you ever wonder how it all got so... complicated?"

Juliette glanced up from her phone, tilting her head. "What do you mean?"

"All of it," he said, gesturing vaguely toward the window. "The missions, the risks, the choices we make. Sometimes I wonder what it would've been like if I'd taken a different path. Stayed away from all this."

The admission surprised him, but once the words were out, they felt inevitable. Maybe it was the exhaustion, or maybe the nightmare still lingered at the edges of his mind. Either way, it felt easier to say it than hold it in.

Juliette leaned back, pondering Derrick's question. "I think we all do," she said quietly. "But I also think once you step into this world, there's no going back. It's not just about choosing it—it chooses you, too. We're here because we're good at it. Because someone has to be."

Her words hit home, resonating with the quiet truth Derrick rarely let himself acknowledge. No matter how much he longed for the simplicity of life with Lydia and Madeline, the decisions that had led him here had carved out a path that couldn't be undone.

Before the moment could linger, Derrick's phone buzzed. It was a message from Tae.

"Visas are ready. We tracked them to a high-rise in Chelyabinsk. Be careful. There's a lot of security in the area."

CHAPTER 10

They loaded their gear into the SUV under the dim light of early evening, the tension thick between them. Derrick double-checked their supplies while Juliette climbed into the driver's seat, her fingers drumming lightly on the steering wheel as a smirk spread across her face.

"You're not getting behind this wheel again after last time," she teased with a wink.

Derrick grimaced, the memory of his sweaty, nerve-wracking attempt at their previous border crossing still fresh. She had a point—Juliette's knack for slipping through tight situations would be an asset, especially with what lay ahead.

"Yeah, yeah," he muttered, tossing the last bag into the back of the SUV. "Just don't get us killed."

Juliette chuckled, her grin widening as she shifted into gear. "No promises."

They drove in silence for the first stretch as the sun dipped low on the horizon, and a light drizzle started to fall on their windshield. Derrick stared out the side window. His mind raced between the mission, Lydia, and the nightmare.

As they approached the Russian border, Juliette's confidence didn't waver. She had a plan, as always. "Remember, we're newlyweds on an extended road trip. I'll handle the talking."

Derrick smirked despite himself. "You're awfully comfortable in that role."

She shot him a sideways glance, her lips curving into a grin. "I'm a professional, Derrick. You should try it sometime."

The border crossing came into view. The ominous structure stood out amongst the flat wilderness surrounding it. The fences, tall and intimidating, were lined with razor wire, and searchlights swept across the area. Derrick's stomach knotted as they approached.

Juliette slowed the SUV and adjusted her posture, her entire demeanor shifting. She suddenly exuded warmth and charm, leaning slightly out the window as the first guard approached. Derrick marveled at how quickly she could change, becoming someone entirely different.

"Dobryy vecher," Juliette greeted the guard in flawless Russian, handing over their papers with a bright smile. "We've been on the road all day—heading to Chelyabinsk for a bit of sightseeing."

The guard inspected the documents, his stern expression betraying no emotion. Derrick kept his head down, playing the part of the quiet, road-weary husband. He let Juliette do all the talking, hoping her confidence would carry them through.

But the guards weren't buying it.

One gave a curt nod and motioned for them to pull to the side. "Search the vehicle," he ordered.

Derrick's stomach dropped. Juliette's fingers tightened on the wheel, and she glanced at him. No words were needed—they both knew this wasn't good. With a subtle nod, they decided on their next move.

After pulling the vehicle to the side, they grabbed their bags and quietly slipped out of the SUV. Derrick bolted after Juliette, his heart pounding as they wove through the dark terrain. Trees blurred in his peripheral vision, the rough ground testing his every step. Shouts erupted behind them, followed by the sharp crack of branches as their pursuers closed in.

Juliette moved ahead like she'd memorized the landscape, navigating the uneven ground with ease. Derrick struggled to keep up, his boots skidding on the rain-slick earth as the steady drizzle turned into a cold, relentless downpour. His breaths came in quick bursts, mingling with hers as they pushed deeper into the countryside.

After what felt like an eternity, the sounds of pursuit faded into the distance. Only the steady rhythm of raindrops on leaves remained. They slowed to a stop, both of them bent over and gasping for air.

"I think we lost them," Juliette panted, her hands braced on her knees.

Derrick scanned the darkened tree line for any sign of movement. "For now," he said, catching his breath. "We need to find shelter."

They pressed on, moving on into the dense forest. A few minutes later, they stumbled upon a small clearing. Derrick dropped his bag and immediately began gathering fallen branches and leaves, piecing together a makeshift shelter while Juliette worked to clear the ground beneath it. The rain had soaked through his jacket, but keeping busy helped push away the chill seeping into his bones.

Once the shelter was up, Derrick worked quickly to start a small fire. The flickering flames brought much-needed warmth to the cool, damp air. He sat back, feeling a glimmer of relief as the heat began to thaw his frozen fingers.

Juliette scooted closer to the fire, her arms hugging her knees tightly as tremors ran through her body. "S-six hours until daylight," she whispered, her teeth chattering between words. "Might as well g-get some rest."

Derrick nodded in agreement, but as he settled onto the ground, he noticed Juliette shivering. The fire wasn't doing enough to fend off the cold, and her wet clothes weren't helping either. He hesitated for a moment, not entirely comfortable with what he was about to suggest.

"You're freezing," Derrick said, pulling an emergency blanket from his bag. "We should... stay close to conserve heat. No spooning though," he added awkwardly, trying to make light of the situation. "Back to back."

Juliette smirked faintly but didn't respond right away. Instead, she shrugged off her coat and hung it on a stick near the fire to dry. She hesitated briefly, taking a deep breath, before pulling off her shirt and pants, leaving her in nothing but her underwear.

Derrick's eyes darted away, his cheeks flushing.

She wrung out as much water as she could from the damp fabric before setting it aside. Standing barefoot on the freezing ground, she let out a sharp breath, hopping from one foot to the other as the chill bit at her exposed skin. "B-better than c-catching hypothermia," she said, her teeth chattering between words, as shivers racked her body. Without hesitation, she crawled quickly under the blanket, seeking relief from the biting cold.

Derrick, still reluctant, removed his soaked coat and boots, grimacing as the cold air bit at his damp shirt. When he reached for his pants, he hesitated, his hand hovering over the waistband.

Hypothermia can't be that bad... right?

The thought was fleeting, a weak attempt to justify keeping them on, but the chill seeping into his bones told him otherwise. He exhaled sharply, shaking his head. *Come on, Derrick. Get over yourself.*

Juliette noticed his hesitation and arched an eyebrow, her lips twitching into a faint, playful smirk despite her shivering. "Relax," she said, her tone laced with teasing. "I promise, I've seen worse."

With a reluctant sigh, he peeled off his pants, setting them near the fire with the rest of their wet clothes. He slid under the blanket, careful to maintain some semblance of distance. But Juliette had other ideas and pressed her back firmly against his, her shivering body instinctively curling closer to his warmth.

The contact sent a jolt through Derrick, her bare shoulder brushing against his shirt. His breath caught, and he clenched his fists, trying to focus on the uneven ground beneath him instead of the heat radiating from her skin. *This is survival. Nothing more.*

"Better?" he muttered, his voice tinged with embarrassment.

Her breath slowed as the warmth began to seep in. "Much," she said softly, her voice carrying a hint of warmth. "Always prepared, huh, Boy Scout?"

The words hit him harder than she could've known. *Boy Scout.* The nickname stirred a flood of memories—Lydia's voice, her teasing smile, the way she said it with affection woven into every syllable. He closed his eyes, but the memory lingered. *Lydia would understand, wouldn't she? This is just survival. She'd understand.*

Juliette shifted closer, her shivering more pronounced despite the fire's modest warmth. She let out a dramatic sigh, her voice laced with a teasing edge. "I'm *so* cold. Is there anything else you could do to warm me up?"

Derrick didn't miss a beat. "I could set you on fire. That would definitely warm you up," he replied dryly, his tone sharp enough to cut through the chilly air.

Her soft laugh carried a hint of genuine amusement, but she didn't miss the unyielding edge in his voice. *He's going to be a hard nut to crack,* she thought wryly. Still, something about his resolve only intrigued her further.

After a moment, Juliette adjusted her position again, this time pressing the small of her back deliberately against his. The movement was subtle but intentional, and for a fleeting moment, it felt like they fit perfectly, their bodies aligning in a way that blurred the line between necessity and something more.

Derrick's breath hitched, his mind scrambling for a distraction as the intimacy of the moment settled heavily over him. *Maybe hypothermia isn't so bad after all,* he thought grimly, every muscle in his body tensing as though resisting the magnetic pull of her presence.

Feeling his tension, she smiled. *So proper, Derrick. Always the gentleman. Always thinking about her. We'll just see.*

Her fingers brushed the edge of the blanket, her mind wandering. *What would it take to break that loyalty? To make him see me instead of her?* The thought was both thrilling and unsettling, and she quickly shoved it aside. But the idea lingered, a small seed taking root.

The rain's steady rhythm outside and the fire's gentle crackling lulled her closer to sleep, yet Derrick's quiet strength held her attention. *That kind of loyalty, that kind of presence—it's rare. Maybe even worth pursuing.* She shifted again, her movements deliberate this time. "You're awfully tense for someone sharing a blanket," she said softly, the teasing lilt returning to her voice.

Derrick exhaled sharply. "We're cold, tired, and stuck in the middle of nowhere. Excuse me if I'm not exactly comfortable."

Juliette smirked, the tension in his voice revealing more than he intended. "Strong men have their limits too," she whispered, letting the words hang in the air before closing her eyes.

Derrick stared at the fire, its flickering light casting mesmerizing patterns on the shelter walls. His back pressed against Juliette's, their shared warmth the only reprieve from the night's bitter chill. He closed his eyes, picturing Lydia and imagining she was the one lying behind him. Her voice echoed in his mind, steadying him as it always did. *She'd understand. She trusts me.*

But the question lingered: *Would she still trust me if she saw this moment?* The thought twisted in his chest, and he clenched his jaw, willing the doubt away. Sleep crept closer, but his thoughts refused to rest.

Behind him, Juliette stared into the darkness. The rough edge of his back against hers felt far too intimate for comfort, yet she didn't pull away. *Why does this feel so... safe?* She tried to retreat behind the armor she'd perfected over years of undercover work, but Derrick's quiet strength gnawed at her defenses.

As his breathing steadied, the shared warmth between them grew impossible to ignore. For the first time in years, Juliette felt a vulnerability she wasn't sure she wanted to admit.

***

The sun rose above the horizon, painting the sky in soft hues of pink and gold. Despite the light's warmth, the morning chill seeped into Derrick's bones. He stretched, wincing as he worked out the stiffness in his joints from a night on the damp ground. Sliding his pants back on, he made his way to the fire.

Looks like the rain finally stopped, he thought, rubbing his hands together as he crouched near the dying fire. Adding a few more sticks, he tried to coax a bit more heat to dry them out, but the fire flickered weakly and refused to catch as he wished.

Juliette stirred behind him, groaning softly as she pushed herself upright. "Sleeping on the ground... that never gets easier," she said, rolling her neck with a grimace.

"It's like a rite of passage," Derrick replied, tossing a few sticks onto the embers. "One for much younger people, I'm afraid."

He reached into his bag, pulled out two water bottles, and tossed one to her. "Here. It's no coffee, but it'll keep you upright."

Juliette cracked open the bottle and took a long drink. "I'll take what I can get," she replied, her voice still thick with sleep.

Taking a long drink, Juliette grimaced but didn't complain. "I'd kill for coffee right now. And maybe a real bed. This," she gestured at the damp ground, "isn't exactly my ideal way to start the day."

Derrick smirked faintly, unfolding the map from his jacket pocket. "We're about five kilometers from Troitsk," he said after a moment, his finger tracing their route on the map. "If we're lucky, we can get a car or hitch a ride to Chelyabinsk. If not..." He glanced at Juliette. "...it's going to be a very long walk."

Juliette leaned back against the tree trunk, brushing dirt from her damp clothes. "Hot breakfast and dry socks," she said wistfully. "That's all I ask... and maybe not smelling like a swamp."

Derrick turned his attention back to the map in his hands, doing his best to avoid watching. Still, his eyes glanced up once or twice before he caught himself, and he quickly refocused on the map, clearing his throat awkwardly. Juliette, ever perceptive, noticed but said nothing, her lips curving into the faintest smirk as she pulled her jeans on and zipped them up.

She began packing their gear, shaking off the remnants of sleep. Derrick scanned the surroundings and plotted their course in his head. Troitsk wasn't far, but the Russian border checkpoint had left him uneasy. They needed to stay low, and any attention drawn to them could be disastrous.

"We'll stick to the tree line as much as possible," Derrick said, folding the map and tucking it into his jacket pocket. "No open roads until we know what we're walking into."

Juliette tightened the straps of her pack and gave him a teasing grin. "Lead the way, boy scout."

That nickname. It always landed differently, tugging at memories he couldn't afford to dwell on. Lydia's voice echoed in his mind, teasing him the same way. The warmth of her laugh felt close enough to touch, but it only left a hollow ache in its place. Shaking it off, he nodded and set out.

What little was left of the fire was doused quickly, and their tracks brushed away as best as they could manage. Morning air hung crisp and still, the faint rustle of leaves the only sound accompanying their footsteps. The forest felt both protective and confining, its canopy sheltering them from view but also hiding what might lie ahead.

After an hour of walking, the faint outline of Troitsk appeared on the horizon. Derrick stopped, scanning the area carefully for any sign of military patrols or police.

Juliette stepped beside him. "So far, so good," she said quietly.

Derrick nodded, keeping his eyes on the town. "Let's hope our luck holds."

The road into Troitsk was quiet, the town gradually revealing itself as the sun climbed higher in the sky. Narrow roads wound through clusters of simple, weathered buildings. Wooden fences and faded shop signs hinted at a place more concerned with practicality than charm.

At the edge of town, a small restaurant caught their attention. The aroma of coffee and fresh bread drifted through the open door, enough to lure them inside. A few locals occupied the tables, their conversations laid back. They slid into a corner booth keeping their movements natural. The waitress, a woman in her fifties with kind eyes, greeted them with a smile that eased some of Derrick's tension.

Breakfast came quickly—eggs and crusty, freshly made bread. But the coffee was the real reward. As soon as Derrick took his first sip, warmth spread through his body, soothing his bones and rejuvenating him after the cold, grueling night in the countryside. Across from him, Juliette cradled her cup, her shoulders visibly relaxing as she let out a soft sigh.

For a while, they ate in companionable silence, the exhaustion from the previous day settling in now that the adrenaline had faded. Derrick's mind churned, already mapping their next steps, while Juliette seemed content to savor the brief comfort.

"This almost feels normal," she said as she broke off a piece of bread.

Derrick gave a faint nod, his lips quirking into a small smile, but his thoughts stayed ahead of the moment.

After breakfast, they paid their bill and slipped out, keeping a low profile as they made their way through the streets. They stopped at a modest clothing shop, purchasing a few simple items—fresh shirts, pants, warm jackets and, to Juliette's delight, dry socks.

Continuing on, they reached a small rental car agency a few blocks away. The woman at the desk barely glanced at them as they handed over their passports—no questions, no suspicious looks, just the keys to an old but reliable sedan and a full gas tank. As they drove away from Troitsk and headed for Chelyabinsk, Derrick's grip on the steering wheel finally began to relax.

By the time they pulled into the parking lot of the *Radisson Blu* in Chelyabinsk, the sun was high in the afternoon sky. The towering building stood out like a rescue beacon for Derrick's aching body.

"Am I going to have to carry you to the room?" Juliette joked.

Derrick rolled his eyes, but then paused, contemplating how it might not be the worst idea she had come up with.

After washing up, Derrick gathered their dirty clothes into a bag and headed down to the laundry room while Juliette took her turn in the shower.

He loaded the washer and sat down on one of the hard plastic chairs. The whir of the machine made his eyes heavy. Derrick let his eyes drift closed, his body finally succumbing to the fatigue of the past few days. He jolted awake at the sound of the dryer buzzer, disoriented for a moment before grabbing the warm, freshly dried clothes.

When he returned to the room, the smell of hotel shampoo filled the air. Juliette was standing by the mirror, a towel draped over her shoulders as she dried her hair.

"Smelling like a swamp is so last season," Derrick said, his voice light but edged with tired humor.

Juliette turned, tossing the towel onto the bed with a grin. "Says the man who could give me a run for my money last night. I was starting to think you were part bog."

Dinner in the hotel's dining area provided a quiet reprieve. They chose a corner table near the windows where the golden light from the setting sun filtered through the glass, softening the room's aura.

Juliette leaned forward, her voice low, "Tomorrow, we'll need to—"

Derrick shook his head subtly, cutting her off. "Not here," he said, keeping his tone casual. "Too many ears."

Juliette nodded and changed the subject. "Thank you for last night," she said, meeting his eyes. "I know it was uncomfortable for you, but I think I would have frozen if we hadn't shared that blanket. What do you think Lydia would think about last night?"

The question stopped him mid-bite. He set his fork down slowly, giving her a confident look. "It was survival. She'd understand. She trusts me."

Juliette raised her brows slightly, as if she'd expected something different. "Trust like that isn't exactly common," she explained, her voice barely above a whisper. Her gaze lingered on her plate, and for a moment, something flickered in her expression. She wasn't sure what answer she wanted, but his calm certainty unsettled her in a way she hadn't anticipated.

Derrick shifted in his seat as he took a drink of his water. "It's not just trust. It's... knowing someone. Deeply. That's why I can do this job and still go home with my head held high."

The conviction in his voice stung more than she'd expected. She nodded absently, brushing her fingers along the rim of her glass, buying herself a moment. "She's lucky to have you," she said softly, her words slipping out before she could think better of it. Her eyes met his for a heartbeat before flicking back down. That small admission felt too raw, too much like revealing her hand.

His response annoyed her more. "You've met her. I'm the lucky one!"

Juliette resisted the urge to roll her eyes and redirected the conversation with a faint laugh. "Not many people would have made that offer and been such a gentleman."

Derrick shrugged, brushing it off. "Boy scout, remember? Besides, I couldn't just let you freeze... who else would keep me out of trouble?"

CHAPTER 11

It was around midnight when a sharp noise broke the stillness of the room. Derrick's eyes flew open as the door swung inward, and several men stepped inside. Dressed in dark jackets, their badges caught the dim light, gleaming coldly. Their expressions were stern and professional—Russian intelligence agents.

Juliette stirred beside him, her body tensing as she realized what was happening. "What the—?" she whispered, throwing off the covers and starting to rise.

"Stay down," Derrick said. "Let them do their job."

She glared at him, clearly ready to attack the first man who came too close, but Derrick shook his head lightly. This was Russia, and the FSB didn't bother with subtlety. They were thorough, invasive, and always watching.

One of the men, clearly the leader, stepped forward while the others began searching the room. They rummaged through luggage, checked drawers, and flipped through personal belongings without hesitation. The leader's eyes swept the room, landing on Derrick and Juliette, his scrutiny sharp enough to make the air feel heavier.

"So," the officer said, his Russian accent thick, each word deliberate. "You say you are newlyweds, yes?" His gaze shifted to the two separate beds, his brow raising in suspicion. "Strange. Not like couple in love. Why you sleep apart?"

Juliette froze, clearly scrambling for a response. The reality of the situation hit her hard, and he could see hesitation flicker in her eyes.

Derrick, however, was prepared. With a sigh, he rolled his eyes and shot her an exasperated look. "We had a fight," he said sharply, his voice laced with frustration. "I called her mother overweight and she's been mad at me since yesterday, so we ended up in separate beds. Couples argue. You've been married, right?" letting the rhetorical question hang.

The officer studied them, his skepticism unshaken. He motioned to one of his men, who handed him their passports. Flipping through them, he frowned. "No entry stamps for Russia," he noted, his voice dangerously calm. "How you explain that?"

"We've been hiking," Derrick replied, his tone even but with just the right edge of frustration. "Through multiple countries. Didn't realize we'd crossed into Russia until we got into town. Thought we were still in Kazakhstan. Honest mistake."

The officer's lips pressed into a thin line, his eyes narrowing. Derrick kept his expression steady, his body language projecting irritation rather than guilt. It was a game he'd played before—pushing just enough to seem truthful but not enough to escalate the situation.

After a few more tense questions, the officer gave a curt nod to his team. They finished their search without a word, finding nothing suspicious. Tucking the passports into his jacket pocket, the leader stepped back. "We watch you," he said coldly before turning on his heel and leaving the room. "Everything. Always."

The others followed, the door closing with a quiet click.

Derrick exhaled slowly, leaning back against the headboard as he glanced at Juliette. "We need to be more convincing," he said quietly. "They're going to monitor everything now. That includes what happens in here."

Juliette raised an eyebrow, her tone light but probing. "And by that, you mean...?"

"They'll bug the room. Cameras, microphones. If we don't act like a married couple, they'll know something's off."

For a moment, she kept a straight face, but then a flicker of amusement crossed her features. "So... we're sharing a bed now?"

Derrick's grimace spoke volumes. "We don't have a choice," he replied flatly, his voice clipped with reluctance. "They're looking for any excuse to detain us."

Juliette's lips curved into a faint smirk, though her thoughts betrayed more than she let on. He wasn't giving her much to work with, not even a flicker of acknowledgment at her attempts to push the boundaries. Most men in his position would at least react, but Derrick stayed infuriatingly composed. It was starting to chip away at her carefully built defenses, leaving her questioning why his indifference bothered her so much.

But Derrick's discomfort grew. He wasn't sure if it was being trapped in Russia, monitored by a hostile intelligence agency, or that Juliette seemed to be enjoying this part of the charade a little too much.

"Get some sleep," Derrick sighed, pulling the covers up and turning away from her. "We have a long day ahead of us."

Juliette hesitated. "I thought we were supposed to be sleeping together now?"

"We don't start that until tomorrow, remember? Your mom's fat and you're mad at me."

Juliette gasped. "She is not, tu crétes!"

Derrick chuckled. "At least you have the mad part down."

***

After grabbing a quick breakfast, they set out for the high-rise where the truck had last been seen. The building loomed over the town, a towering 30-story structure with glass windows that reflected the pale morning sky. Inside, it housed a mix of businesses—law firms, accounting offices, small tech startups, and foreign companies. Finding Arabella in such a place would be like searching for a needle in a haystack.

Derrick paused just outside the entrance, scanning the building from top to bottom. "This is going to be a challenge," he groaned. "Especially since we're outsiders."

Juliette nodded. "Do we have anything to narrow it down?"

"I did some research last night," Derrick said, pulling a folded sheet of paper from his jacket. "Ruled out the legitimate businesses. That leaves only a handful of questionable ones." He handed the list to Juliette, who scanned it quickly.

"At least it's a start," she remarked, tucking the list into her pocket. "Let's get to it."

Hours dragged as they checked the offices one by one. Juliette handled most of the talking, slipping effortlessly into different personas—a prospective client here, a courier there—while Derrick scanned the spaces for any signs of Arabella. The deeper they dug, the more Derrick's irritation grew.

By mid-afternoon, they regrouped back in the lobby, both looking worn and discouraged. Derrick shook his head. "She's not here."

Juliette leaned against a marble column, shaking her head. "It was worth a shot."

With no leads left in the building, they walked to a nearby park to regroup. The park was open and quiet, with only a few people scattered about. It seemed like the perfect spot to make a secure call without drawing attention. Derrick found a shaded bench beneath a large oak tree, glanced around to ensure no one was watching, and dialed Tae's number.

He answered on the second ring, his voice tense. "You find anything?"

Derrick exhaled, staring at the expanse of grass before him. "Nothing useful. We spent hours combing through that building where the truck was last spotted, but Arabella's not there. Came up empty."

There was a pause on the other end before Tae replied, "All right, I'll go over the satellite images again. Maybe we missed something."

"Good luck," Derrick said dryly. "We're not going far without our passports, anyway."

Tae let out a short laugh. "Let me guess— Russian intelligence got involved?"

"You could say that. They raided our room last night, searched everything, and asked a few questions. Didn't find anything to hold us on, but we're definitely under surveillance now."

"That's a problem," Tae said quietly. "I'll work on getting you some backup. Let me see if I can cut through the red tape and get your passports back."

"Appreciate it," Derrick said, glancing at Juliette, who was scanning the park with a watchful eye. "But make it quick. Every minute we lose, Arabella gets further away."

Tae's voice was firm. "We'll find her, Derrick. Sit tight for a few hours. I'll get back to you as soon as I have something."

"We'll be waiting," Derrick replied, ending the call. He shoved the phone back into his pocket, his frustration mounting.

Juliette turned to him, one eyebrow raised. "What now?"

"We wait," he said with a sigh. "Tae's rechecking the satellite footage. Hopefully, we missed something."

Juliette tilted her head, studying him for a moment. "You hate waiting."

"Definitely not my strong suit," he admitted.

***

Evening settled over the town. Derrick checked his phone for what felt like the hundredth time that day—still no word from Tae. Frustration simmered beneath the surface, but he knew impatience wouldn't help. The mission came first, and right now, their best option was to blend in and avoid suspicion.

Juliette sat on the windowsill, one knee pulled to her chest as she stared out at the quiet street below. "We can't just sit here," she said finally, her voice sharp and impatient. "It's not exactly what a couple on their honeymoon would do."

Derrick nodded, knowing she was right. If Russian agents were watching them, they had to sell their cover as newlyweds. And that meant doing what newlyweds would do.

"Let's get out of here," Derrick said, glancing at his watch. "Dinner. Something normal."

Juliette's lips curved into a faint smile. "Normal for a newly married couple means romantic, right?"

He ignored the teasing, already heading to his bag for a fresh shirt. "Let's just sell the part."

After a quick shower and change of clothes, they left the hotel and headed toward an upscale restaurant in town. As they walked down the quiet street, Juliette glanced at Derrick and smiled, "You know, newlyweds hold hands." Derrick hesitated for a moment before reaching out awkwardly, his fingers brushing hers. Her smirk grew as she took his hand, her grip softer than he expected. "See? That wasn't so hard."

Derrick groaned a little. "Let's just get through dinner. The more convincing we are, the safer we'll be."

Inside the restaurant, soft lighting glinted off wine glasses, and the low hum of conversation filled the air. The waiter led them to a table in the back, where a single candle flickered between them. Derrick slid into his seat, eyes scanning the room before settling on the menu in front of him.

"I'll have the chicken and rice," he said simply as he handed the menu back. Juliette, however, was more animated. She ordered a bottle of wine with her meal, flashing the waiter a warm smile that seemed to soften even his professional demeanor.

The bottle arrived with a quiet clink of glass on the table, and Juliette poured herself a generous amount before swirling it in her glass. "If we're going to play the part," she said lightly, "we might as well enjoy it." She took a sip, her eyes flicking to Derrick.

A small shrug was all he gave in response, though he occasionally mirrored her subtle gestures—brushing his fingers over hers or holding her hand when it felt necessary. His focus kept drifting to the rest of the room, instincts on high alert, scanning for anything out of place.

"What kind of honeymoon do you think we'd have?" she asked, the question catching him mid-thought. Her voice carried a teasing edge, but her gaze lingered a second too long, giving away something deeper.

"That's not worth imagining," he replied. The words came easily, but a slight furrow in his brow betrayed his discomfort. He took a sip of water, not meeting her gaze. "We're here for the job."

The corner of her mouth twitched, almost forming a smile before she quickly looked away. "Relax, Honey. Just trying to keep the act convincing."

She took another sip of wine, the heat from the alcohol making her feel bolder than she intended. She glanced at Derrick, catching the way his jaw tightened slightly whenever she leaned in too close or let her fingers linger on his. He was focused, disciplined, and completely unaware of how much space he'd started to occupy in her mind. It frustrated her as much as it thrilled her.

You're letting this get to you, she reminded herself. *Focus. He's not for you.*

Her gaze softened as she traced the rim of her glass. "Do you think Lydia knows how lucky she is?" The question slipped out before she could stop herself.

Derrick's hand froze halfway to his glass. His eyes lifted, studying her carefully now. "What do you mean by that?"

"She has someone who would risk everything for her," Juliette said quietly. Her gaze dropped back to her plate, but the weight of her words lingered. "That kind of loyalty... it's rare."

He leaned forward slightly, studying her face for a moment. "She's my wife. That's how it's supposed to be."

A faint, bitter laugh escaped her lips as she swirled the wine again. "You make it sound so simple."

"It is," Derrick said firmly, though a flicker of doubt crossed his mind. *Was this part of the act, or something else entirely? Her tone, her expression—both felt too genuine, like they came from a place she couldn't quite hide.*

"Fair enough," she said softly, her voice quieter now. The edges of her mask were slipping, and she knew it. The wine wasn't helping. Neither was the warmth in his eyes when he wasn't looking away.

The rest of the meal passed with careful conversation, both treading lightly as if aware of the other's tension. Derrick focused on finishing his plate, his mind already shifting back to the mission. Across the table, Juliette let her guard down just enough to steal glances at him when he wasn't looking, her thoughts veering into territory she didn't want to explore.

By the time they left the restaurant, the air between them had shifted—neither ready to acknowledge it, but both unable to ignore it. Derrick held the door open as Juliette stepped out, her smile fleeting but genuine.

After dinner, they walked back to the hotel in silence. Juliette didn't even remember she was supposed to be holding his hand.

Derrick changed and headed down to the pool to do some laps. Juliette followed, heading to the hot tub with a glass of wine. She slipped into the bubbling water with a sigh that could have been mistaken for genuine relaxation. She leaned back, letting the steam rise around her.

In the pool, Derrick started his laps. The steady rhythm of his strokes was more than exercise—it was a way to think without distractions. Every pull of his arms through the water felt like a deliberate push against the noise in his head.

Her eyes followed him, the wine glass forgotten for a moment. The way he moved effortlessly through the water stirred something she didn't want to name. *This is dangerous.* The thought flitted through her mind, uninvited but persistent. Letting her feelings take root wasn't part of the plan, but lately, her thoughts kept drifting to him, no matter how hard she tried to focus. *Remember your mission.*

When Derrick finished his laps, he paused at the edge of the hot tub, droplets rolling off his shoulders as he caught his breath. The hesitation before he slipped into the warm water didn't go unnoticed.

The moment he eased in, the heat began working on the stiffness in his muscles, but the tension in his chest refused to budge. *She's watching me again*, he realized, catching her gaze just as she turned back to her glass.

"You know," Juliette began, "I've noticed those scars before. The burns. Seems like there's a story behind them."

Derrick flexed his fingers, his eyes following the faint, jagged lines that marred his skin. "It's nothing," he said, brushing her off. His voice came out flat, but the crack in his armor was obvious, even to him. He then let out a short, humorless laugh. "Just another work injury."

Juliette wasn't so easily deterred. Her tone softened. "Come on, Derrick. Scars like that don't come from punching a clock."

He exhaled, leaning back against the edge of the hot tub as if the water could somehow dilute the memory. "It was a few years ago," he began, his voice quieter now. "Emily—my flight medic—was in a crash. Her helicopter went down. I tried to pull her out, but…" He trailed off, the memory vivid and raw. "I wasn't fast enough. Got these for my trouble."

Juliette's expression softened, her eyes glinting with sadness. "I'm sorry," she said, her voice barely above a whisper. "You must've been close."

"In that line of work, you don't have a choice," he said, his gaze fixed on the ripples in the water. "She was my partner. Her husband and kids… we were friends too." A faint smile crossed his lips, tinged with sadness. "You get close because you have to. And because it's impossible not to."

Juliette studied his face. "Did you ever… want more with her?" she asked cautiously.

Derrick's mind drifted. The late-night laughs, quiet conversations, the kind of bond born out of life-and-death situations. "Maybe in another life," he admitted after a pause. "But she was happy, and I wasn't about to cross that line. I respected her too much for that."

Reaching under the water, Juliette's hand brushed against his lightly before giving it a reassuring squeeze. "Some people just leave marks on us," she said quietly.

Raising his hand, she looked closer at the scars before turning his arm over. Her finger lightly traced up the jagged imperfections that ran along his wrists. "Izzy really did a number on you, didn't she?" The words came so casually, but they hit Derrick like a thunderclap.

His stomach tightened as his mind raced. *I never told her about Izzy.* His hand stiffened slightly in hers, and he tried to pull it back, but she held on just long enough to feel the tension.

"How do you know about her?" His voice came out firmer than Juliette expected.

She let go of his hand, leaning back in surprise. "Tae," she said shakily. "He briefed me after you left for the airport. He thought I should be aware, considering the history there."

Derrick's shoulders eased some, though the alarm in his mind didn't fully quiet. He nodded slowly, his gaze still searching hers for cracks in the explanation. *That tracks*, he told himself, though something about her tone lingered in his mind.

Juliette breathed easier watching him calm, but internally, her thoughts swirled. *That was close. Too close.*

Sinking a little deeper into the warm water, Derrick exhaled. "Yeah," he said finally, "She did."

The arrival of a hotel worker interrupted the moment. The man stood in the doorway, glancing at his watch before addressing them. "Pool's closing."

Derrick nodded and pushed himself up, letting the water stream off his arms. "Probably for the best," he said, glancing at Juliette. "I'm starting to wrinkle."

She laughed softly, but as she followed him out of the water, her gaze lingered on him for a bit longer than necessary. *You're slipping, Juliette.*

After drying off and changing, the two made their way to the hotel bar. Juliette slid onto a barstool with ease, her damp hair falling in loose waves. Derrick joined her, keeping a slight distance as he scanned the room out of habit.

"What'll it be?" the bartender asked, setting down a napkin in front of Juliette.

"Something strong," she replied as a playful smile tugged at her lips.

Derrick ordered a soda, causing Juliette's smirk to widen.

"You're really just sticking with a cola?" she teased, tapping her fingers on the counter.

Lifting his glass in a mock toast, Derrick replied, "Someone has to keep a clear head."

As the evening wore on, Juliette ordered another drink—and then another. Her laughter became freer as she leaned back in her seat, gesturing animatedly as she recounted stories from her earlier assignments.

Derrick listened with a faint smile, though his eyes often darted toward the door or the bartender's movements.

By the time they returned to the room, Juliette was visibly tipsy, her steps uneven, but carrying the same confident energy.

Flopping down on the bed, she propped herself up on her elbows. "That was fun," she said, her words slurring slightly. "Almost like a real vacation."

Derrick leaned against the dresser, shaking his head with a small smirk. "Your standards for vacations are pretty low."

She laughed again, rolling onto her back. "Says the man whose idea of fun is swimming laps alone."

"Swimming doesn't come with a hangover."

Juliette gave an exaggerated groan. "You're such a Boy Scout. No fun at all."

Derrick didn't respond though. His mind had already shifted to the reality of their situation. If the Russians were still watching—and he was sure they were—they'd expect a married couple to act the part, even when the curtains were drawn. That meant no more double beds. No more buffer zones. And definitely no avoiding the tension growing between them.

As he scanned the room, a faint crackle of static drew his attention. It was barely noticeable, blending with the hum of the air conditioner, but it was there. His eyes darted to the corner near the smoke detector, where a tiny, almost imperceptible red light pulsed softly. The realization tightened his jaw. They were, in fact, being watched. Every word. Every move.

Juliette sat up, kicking off her shoes as she began pulling her shirt over her head, showing no concern for modesty.

Realizing she wasn't going to stop there, Derrick quickly turned his back, forcing his mind to something—anything—else. He started folding his clothes and adjusting items around the room.

"Relax," she said with a light teasing in her tone. "It's not like you haven't seen a woman change before. Or are you always this polite?"

As she removed her shorts, she continued, "You know, if we are going to sell this, you might want to stop pretending to be so shy."

"Just keeping it professional," Derrick replied curtly, adjusting items on the nearby table.

He kept his gaze steady on the table until movement in the wall mirror caught his attention. Without meaning to, his eyes flicked up, just as Juliette was slipping into her new shirt. With her arms raised, he caught a fleeting glimpse of her chest. His stomach tightened—not because of what he saw, but because of what he didn't.

"You weren't kidding," Derrick said, his voice carefully neutral. "About the doctor doing a good job."

Juliette froze mid-motion, her fingers hovering over the hem of her shirt as she pulled it down. The pause was so slight that most wouldn't have noticed. But Derrick wasn't most people. His words hung in the air as she resumed dressing with an almost imperceptible tension.

No scar," Derrick added, still not turning around. "That's... rare. Impressive, even."

Juliette laughed lightly, her voice carrying a casual air. "Shea butter does wonders," she said, her tone steady, though Derrick caught the faintest edge to it. "Good surgeons, good aftercare, and voilà. Practically new."

Derrick didn't reply immediately. Instead, he adjusted their gear, his jaw tightening. He had seen surgical scars before—clean ones, messy ones, faint ones—but the complete absence of one was unusual. It wasn't just skill; it was perfection. And it didn't sit right with him.

Juliette continued, her voice dipping into something almost playful. "I'd offer to recommend my surgeon, but I doubt you're in the market. Maybe Lydia would be, though? He does more than just remove them. Early birthday present for you perhaps?"

Derrick stiffened slightly, the mention of Lydia throwing his thoughts into a different direction. He forced a chuckle as the tension in his chest eased. "She doesn't need it," he said firmly, focusing on the table again. "She's perfect the way she is."

"Good answer," Juliette said with a faint smirk, turning away as she took down her hair. But as Derrick turned her words over in his mind, she knew she'd accomplished what she intended. His attention was firmly on Lydia now, his earlier observation forgotten— at least for the moment.

Standing at the edge of the bed, Derrick stared down at it, his thoughts running circles. Every part of this arrangement felt wrong. It went against his instincts, his beliefs, everything that made him who he was. But keeping the illusion intact wasn't just important—it was vital. One slip, one moment of hesitation, and their cover would unravel, putting the mission—and their lives—in jeopardy. *You've done worse for a mission. Just get through this.*

On the other side, Juliette slid into bed with an ease that rattled him even more. Her movements were unhurried, comfortable, as if this were routine. She'd shed her shorts without a second thought, curling up under the blanket in just a tank top and bikini briefs. Her casual demeanor might have fooled an outside observer, but for Derrick, it only deepened the knot in his stomach. "I guess Victoria doesn't have secrets anymore."

Tilting her head, Juliette caught his gaze. "It's not a big deal, Derrick," she slurred slightly. "We're just sleeping. No one's going to know if you keep one foot on the floor."

He exhaled sharply trying to settle himself. The knot tightened further as he slowly climbed in. *Keep it professional. Keep it distant.*

The bed seemed smaller than it had just moments ago as the space between them shrunk with every passing second. To sell the act, he draped an arm loosely around her shoulders. The mechanical gesture was devoid of the warmth it should have carried.

This just doesn't feel natural.

Juliette then rolled onto her side, her face close enough for him to feel the warmth of her breath against his neck. A playful smirk danced across her lips as she whispered, "No goodnight kiss? Remember, they're watching."

Derrick's body tensed as a flood of irritation bubbled beneath the surface. *She's enjoying this too much.*

Letting out a heavier sigh, he leaned in, brushing his lips briefly against hers. It was quick, soft, and carefully orchestrated to look convincing without giving her—or himself—more than necessary. As he pulled back, her eyes fluttered closed, her expression carrying a quiet contentment he didn't want to think about.

The moment was interrupted by the buzz of Derrick's phone on the nightstand. *That timing couldn't have been better*, he thought... until he looked at the phone.

Lydia's name appeared on the screen. "*I know it's late there, Honey*," he read silently, her words playing in his mind. "*I just wanted to check on you. I hope you're doing okay. I love you. Kisses!*"

He shivered all over. Looking back at Juliette, she had rolled over, her back now to him. His thoughts spiraled as guilt swept over him in waves.

"She knows," he whispered under his breath, as a heaviness started in his chest. "I don't know how, but I know she does.

CHAPTER 12

That night, sleep came easily to Derrick, drawing him into a rare dream that wasn't shadowed by the usual nightmares. This one was different—pleasant, even exhilarating.

...Derrick lay on a beach chair, the bright Maldivian sun warming his skin as the waves lapped against the stilts of their bungalow below. The ocean stretched out before him in a shimmering expanse of blue. In the distance, dolphins leapt gracefully from the water, playing in the golden sunlight.

He was back in the Maldives, reliving the happiest moments of his honeymoon with Lydia. The air carried the scent of salt and coconut, a gentle breeze brushing against his face. For the first time in what felt like forever, he felt truly content—at peace.

As he lounged in the sunlight, a figure approached him. They wore a red polka-dot bikini, and their skin glowed in the golden rays. Though her face wasn't visible, Derrick didn't need to see it to know who she was. He felt it in every fiber of his being. It was Lydia. Her presence was unmistakable—familiar, comforting... like home.

She sat down beside him, her warmth radiating as she lay her head softly against his chest. Her touch, her nearness—it anchored him, grounding him in a way nothing else could. It was as though all the chaos, pain, and worry had dissolved under the spell of her embrace.

She shifted closer, snuggling against him with an ease that made him smile. Reaching out to caress her, his hands moved gently over her skin, savoring the softness of her body. She responded by tilting her head up, her lips brushing his cheek before meeting his in a soft, tender kiss. It was slow, deliberate—filled with the kind of love and connection that only they shared.

He held her tighter, deepening the kiss as waves of emotion surged through him. This was his Lydia—the woman he had married, the woman he loved with all his heart, the woman he would do anything to protect...

Suddenly, Derrick woke. The room was pitch dark, and for a moment, he was disoriented, his body still heavy with sleep and the lingering remnants of his dream. The softness beside him registered slowly—someone was lying next to him, just like in the dream. The scent of strawberries overwhelmed his senses.

Without thinking, his hand instinctively reached out, brushing against the soft curve of her waist before pulling her closer. *Lydia.* Her name floated through his mind, the fragments of his dream knitting together—the warmth of her skin, the way her touch always anchored him. He leaned forward, pressing a tender kiss to the curve of her neck, his lips lingering.

They stirred, turning toward him. For a fleeting moment, Derrick felt the same warmth, the same sense of comfort and love he'd experienced in the dream. He pulled her closer to his body, his arms wrapping around her as he felt the heat of her skin against his. His hand moved gently under her shirt, caressing her back in a slow, tender motion. *This is home*, he thought, grounding himself in the illusion.

"Derrick," came the whisper, soft and full of invitation as she returned the embrace, wrapping her arms around him.

"Lydia," he whispered, his voice low, almost inaudible. Their lips met, the kiss deepening, consuming. For a moment, it felt perfect.

Then, the cracks appeared.

The response wasn't quite right, the texture of her lips unfamiliar. A current of wrongness broke through the haze, snapping him into the present. His eyes shot open, his breath catching in his throat.

It wasn't Lydia.

Juliette's face hovered inches from his, her eyes wide with a mixture of surprise and desire.

He jerked back as if burned, the name catching in his throat like a razor. "Juliette…" The word came out broken, raw with disbelief and horror. His pulse hammered in his ears as he scrambled backward, yanking at the sheets that tangled around his legs. The edge of the bed gave way beneath him, and he tumbled to the floor with a muffled thud. Panic drove him to his knees, but with the room engulfed in darkness, it was a maze of unseen obstacles.

As he tried to stand, his foot caught on the other bedframe, sending him sprawling out on the floor again.

"Derrick!" Juliette yelled, trying to cut through the chaos.

But Derrick was desperate to push himself away further, clawing at the carpet like he could will the room to stretch wider. His chest heaved as the guilt suffocated him in panic. *Why? How? What just happened?!?* The questions screamed in his head louder than the sound of his body colliding with the furniture.

The room suddenly flooded with light.

Juliette stood by the switch, her tank top wrinkled, her hair disheveled, and her eyes wide with confusion. The blanket hung loosely around her shoulders, half-draped like she hadn't fully grasped what was happening. But it wasn't her state that froze Derrick mid-crawl—it was the way she looked at him.

"Derrick..." Her voice softened, seeing him on all fours like a terrified animal. His body tremored as his gaze darted toward her. It was haunted and hollow. He then snapped away again, unable to hold her stare as he curled up into the corner of the room.

"I... I thought—" His words faltered, tumbling into a silence too heavy to fill. *No excuses. There aren't any. This can't be undone.*

Derrick's chest tightened further as Lydia's voice echoed in his mind from her earlier text: "I hope you're doing okay. I love you!" *How can I face her now?*

Juliette took a hesitant step forward as if she wasn't sure whether to approach or stay back. "Derrick, it's okay." She said quietly.

"No! No, it's not," Derrick snapped, more to himself than her. "It's not okay. None of this is okay!"

He grabbed the spare blanket from the bed and muttered, "I'll take the chair for the rest of the night."

Without waiting for a response, he moved to the armchair near the window, draped the blanket over himself, and sat in the darkness.

"Derrick, can we talk about this?" Juliette pleaded.

The blanket on the chair shook its head.

Juliette sat back down on the bed and typed out a message on her phone. "Plan A is a bust. Plan B is a go."

Moments later, a reply came. "Name the time and place."

***

The next morning, Derrick heard his phone vibrating on the nightstand. He blinked groggily, still disoriented from the events of the night before. Slipping out from the blanket, his gaze shifted to the bed where Juliette lay curled up under the covers. The memory of what had transpired churned in his stomach, but he forced it aside and reached for the phone.

It was Tae.

Answering quickly, he kept his voice low. "Yeah?"

"Derrick, we've got something," Tae said. "After going over the satellite footage again, we tracked a vehicle leaving the compound in Kostanay. It headed to the airport."

Derrick sat up, his focus sharpening. "Go on."

"A plane took off from there and landed in Bucharest, Romania. That's where the trail goes cold. They entered the terminal, but the security footage isn't giving us much to work with after that."

Derrick ran a hand over his face in frustration. "So, she could still be in Bucharest, or she could already be gone."

"Exactly," Tae replied. "We're trying to determine their next move. As of now, we've lost visual, but we're working on it."

Derrick nodded to himself, weighing their next steps. Romania wasn't exactly close, but without their passports, getting there would be nearly impossible. "Any progress on the passports?"

Tae exhaled heavily, his frustration evident. "The State Department is negotiating with the Russians, but it could take weeks to get them released. The bureaucracy's a mess, and they're dragging their feet."

"Weeks?" Derrick's voice sharpened, laced with anger. "Arabella doesn't have weeks, Tae. None of us do."

"I know," he replied quickly. "But there's another option," pausing as if considering his next words carefully. "If you can get to Moscow, we can print new passports for you at the Embassy. It's risky, but it's doable. Once you're there, we can handle the paperwork."

Derrick frowned as his thoughts raced. Moscow was a long way off, but it was faster than waiting for the Russian government to wade through red tape. "How long would it take?"

"If you leave today, you could reach Moscow by tomorrow. We'll have the documents ready, and you'd be back on your way in hours. But..." Tae hesitated, "if Russian authorities catch wind of you traveling without proper papers, it could complicate things even further."

The risk was clear. Traveling through Russia without passports was like painting a target on their backs. But the alternative—sitting in the hotel while Arabella remained missing—was unthinkable.

"Do we have any other choice?" Derrick asked, already knowing the answer.

"Not if you want to move anytime soon," Tae admitted. "I'll set everything up. If you decide to go, stay under the radar. Tourists, plain and simple."

Derrick let out a slow breath, glancing out the window as the pale light of dawn crept over the horizon. "I'll talk to Juliette."

"Let me know when you're on your way," Tae instructed. "I'll ensure everything's ready at the consulate."

"And Tae," Derrick added, "make sure we're not wasting time. We need to find Arabella."

"We're doing everything we can," Tae reassured him. "I'll update you as soon as we have more intel. In the meantime, keep your heads down."

The call ended, and Derrick sat for a moment, processing the plan. Now, they had to figure out how to make it to Moscow without attracting unwanted attention. His gaze shifted back to Juliette, still fast asleep, unaware of the dangerous road ahead.

Derrick stared out the window, his thoughts churning as the plan took shape. Waiting any longer wasn't an option. Staying here would only attract more attention—especially if the FSB had seen what happened last night. The risk wasn't just to the mission now; it was to their lives.

Taking a steadying breath, he crossed the room to where Juliette lay curled under the blankets. He hesitated briefly before nudging her shoulder. "Juliette," he said quietly. "Wake up."

She stirred with a groan, blinking up at him groggily. Her expression tightened as confusion flickered across her face. "What's going on?" she mumbled, sitting up and rubbing her eyes.

"We need to move," Derrick said, his voice firm. "I just talked to Tae. We have a plan, but there's not much time."

Juliette's expression shifted as she focused on his tone. The urgency in his words pulled her fully awake. "What plan?" she asked, her voice sharper now.

Derrick sat down on the edge of the bed, his expression tense. "Tae found something. Arabella was flown out of Kostanay. The plane landed in Bucharest, Romania, but they lost the trail at the airport."

"Romania?" Juliette repeated, sitting straighter as her mind raced. A sharp curse escaped under her breath.

"There's more," Derrick added, lowering his voice and glancing toward the door as though expecting someone to burst in. "Our passports are still tied up in Russian red tape. Tae said it could take weeks for the State Department to sort it out."

Her expression darkened. "We don't have weeks."

"Exactly," Derrick said. "Tae has another idea. If we can get to Moscow, the U.S. Embassy can issue new passports. We could be out of here and in Romania by tomorrow."

Juliette mulled it over, the plan sinking in. A flicker of doubt crossed her face. "It's risky. Traveling across Russia without passports? That's like walking through a minefield."

"I know," Derrick said. "But after last night, staying here isn't an option."

A heavy sigh escaped her as she swung her legs out of bed. "Moscow it is, then. How do we get there?"

"By train," he said. "It keeps us off the radar. Flying's out without passports, and driving would take too long."

"Train works," she said with a curt nod. "When do we leave?"

"As soon as we're ready. Pack light. Tae will have everything set at the consulate when we arrive."

Juliette stood, stretching as she shook off the last remnants of sleep. "All right. Let's move."

They packed quickly, shoving their belongings into their bags and double-checking the room to ensure nothing was left behind. Every move carried a quiet urgency.

As Juliette zipped her bag shut, she glanced over at Derrick. "You think this will work?"

"It has to," Derrick said simply. "We don't have any other options."

CHAPTER 13

The streets bustled with early morning commuters as Derrick and Juliette maneuvered through the crowd toward the train station. Heads down, their brisk pace helped them blend in seamlessly. The last thing they needed was to draw attention before boarding.

Inside the station, Derrick approached the ticket counter. His fluent Russian made the process smooth, even in the midst of the station's chaotic flow of travelers. Within minutes, he returned with two tickets in hand. Juliette lingered near the large windows, her gaze sweeping over the platforms for anything unusual.

"We're on the 10:45 to Moscow," Derrick said, handing her one of the tickets. "I got us a sleeper car. It's a long ride, and we'll need the rest. Plus, the door locks—it'll help us stay off anyone's radar."

Juliette nodded, her fingers brushing the edge of the ticket. "Good thinking."

When their train finally arrived, Derrick and Juliette boarded and navigated the narrow corridor, their bags brushing against the walls. When they located their room, Derrick opened the door, stepping aside to let Juliette enter first.

The room was small, with just enough space for a pair of benches that converted to beds, a fold-out table, and a window that framed the station's activity. Derrick tossed his bag onto the left bench and took a moment to glance around. It wasn't much, but it was private enough to keep them out of sight.

Juliette set her bag down and fiddled with the strap. She glanced around the compartment, darting briefly between the bunks and then to the window as though gauging their surroundings. Derrick caught the small pauses in her movements that didn't match her usual confidence. Something was slightly off, but he couldn't put his finger on it.

The train shuttered to life as it slowly crawled out of the station beginning their thirty-hour journey.

Juliette leaned against the window, watching the platform disappear. As the train picked up speed, she turned and spotted the mini bar tucked beneath the small table.

"Look at that," she said, a spark of mischief lighting her eyes. "We should celebrate. Vodka seems fitting for the occasion since we're in Russia, don't you think?"

Derrick shook his head. "I'll pass."

Juliette tilted her head, her tone playful. "I know you're not much of a drinker, but you've never said why."

"Had a bad experience last time," Derrick replied flatly, hoping to end the conversation there.

"Come on," Juliette pressed, her smile widening. "It'll take the edge off. We're stuck on this train for thirty hours. Might as well make the most of it. Besides, it might help you sleep."

Derrick hesitated. The memory of Izzy's vicious torturing flashed through his mind. Still, the persistent look in Juliette's eyes wore him down. With a sigh, he finally relented. "Fine. One drink."

Juliette grinned triumphantly, retrieving a small bottle from the mini bar. She poured two drinks and handed one to him. "To getting out of Chelyabinsk," she said, raising her cup.

Derrick clinked his drink against hers and took a sip. The vodka burned going down, but the heat wasn't unpleasant. He set the cup down, confident one drink wouldn't do much.

Juliette leaned back against the tiny compartment's wall, her legs tucked beneath her on the narrow seat. She swirled the vodka in her glass lazily before speaking. "What was your most memorable mission?"

Resting his elbows on the table, Derrick thought about it. "Most memorable..." he echoed, his voice trailing off as he searched his mind. After a moment, he sat up straighter, a faint smirk tugging at the corner of his mouth. "Tripoli," he said simply. "That one tops the list."

Juliette raised an eyebrow. "Tripoli? That was horribly boring when I went. What happened with you?"

"It was chaos!" Derrick began, leaning back against the wall. "It started out like a normal tour. I was bored one day, so I took a trashcan and made an 'automatic dispenser' for my phosphamite compound I developed in school. It was something I thought might come in handy if we ever had to evacuate somewhere quickly. Never dreamed I'd actually use it."

Juliette leaned in, "Let me top off your glass," as she filled Derrick's cup.

Without thinking, Derrick took a quick sip before continuing. "Well, our base was attacked and we had to leave quickly. I set off the device before running out. A white beam of plasma shot out the front door, knocking down one of the guards named Obadiah. He almost got impaled by the beam!"

Juliette's grip tightened on her glass, whitening her knuckles for a second before she took another sip. Her demeanor changed ever so slightly, but it was enough Derrick caught it.

"Something wrong?" he asked.

Juliette blinked as her smile quickly returned. "No, just... that's insane. I can't believe you walked out of that alive."

Juliette, as if sensing his lingering unease, leaned forward and held up the bottle. "Sounds like a story worth toasting to," she said lightly, filling her glass and motioning toward his. "Another drink?"

He hesitated, his earlier suspicion mixing with a growing sense of discomfort. "I think I've had enough."

"Come on," she coaxed, her tone playful but insistent. "Just one more. You can't not toast to a story like that!"

Derrick sighed, sliding his glass toward her. One more, but that's it."

Juliette smiled as she poured, her casual demeanor firmly back in place. Derrick accepted the glass but kept his eyes on her, his thoughts churning even as the vodka burned its way down his throat. Something about her reaction didn't sit right, but the haze of the alcohol made it hard for him to think.

CHAPTER 14

Derrick lay back on the bench. His head was now swimming, and his eyelids heavy. Closing them, he hoped sleep would come quickly... or at least before the vodka decided to come back up.

Juliette announced that she was going to go and find some snacks before slipping out, leaving Derrick alone with his spinning room.

The corridor was quiet as she made her way to the next car. Once out of earshot, she pulled out her phone, her demeanor shifting. Dialing a number, she brought the phone to her ear and waited for the connection.

When she spoke, her voice was cold and detached, a sharp contrast to the warmth she had shown Derrick moments earlier. "Arabella is in Bucharest. Plan B is in play. Fifteen minutes." She ended the call without another word.

Juliette slipped back into the room. "They don't have anything out until lunch," she said as she took a seat next to the window. Derrick barely acknowledged her, head still spinning from the vodka.

A small, almost imperceptible grin tugged at the corner of her lips before her attention shifted back to her phone.

Minutes passed as the sound of Derrick's snoring started to grate on Juliette's nerves. Then, without warning, a jolt shook the entire car. The train screeched violently as the sound of metal against metal filled the air. Derrick bolted upright as the train ground to a halt.

Juliette sprang to the window, and her face paled as several military vehicles sped toward the train, dust billowing in their wake, obscuring the horizon. "They found us!" she shouted, her eyes wide with panic. "We need to go, now!"

Derrick stumbled to his feet, the world spinning around him. "Go where? We're on a train in the middle of nowhere... surrounded!"

Juliette ignored him, her fingers flying over her phone. "This is Agent Rousseau. Interpol team, requesting immediate airlift at my coordinates. Priority extract!" Her voice carried an authority Derrick hadn't heard before adding to his confusion.

"If that was an option, why didn't we do this from the start?" His voice cracked with frustration as he struggled to keep up.

She didn't answer, only grabbing his arm with a force that startled him. "We don't have time for this! We need to move!" Tugging him toward the exit, she yanked the door open, letting the blinding sunlight pour into the cramped space.

Between the train cars, ladders stretched toward the roof. Juliette ascended without hesitation.

"Get up here!" she called, her voice cutting through the roar of the wind.

Derrick climbed after her, and just as his feet hit the roof, the unmistakable thrum of helicopter blades filled the air. His hair whipped around his head as the unmarked aircraft descended, its rotor wash scattering dirt and debris across the roof of the train.

Juliette scrambled aboard the helicopter first, turning to extend her hand to Derrick. The moment their hands clasped, her grip felt deliberate—too deliberate. Derrick's gaze flicked to her face, and his stomach dropped as the helicopter started ascending. Her expression wasn't relief. It was something else entirely. Cold. Calculating.

A chill ran through him as time seemed to slow. The roar of the wind faded into the background as he locked eyes with her. Panic surged in his chest as her grip began to loosen.

"Juliette..." he breathed, disbelief freezing him in place.

Her smirk was barely there, but it was unmistakable—a cruel, fleeting acknowledgment of what she was about to do. With one final, deliberate movement, she let go.

The fall was immediate. Derrick's body slammed onto the roof of the train car with a bone-jarring thud, the impact tearing the breath from his lungs. Pain seared through his side as he rolled, gravity pulling him toward the edge. He clawed at the slick surface, but it was no use. He tumbled over the side, landing hard on the cold ground below.

Stars burst behind his eyes as he tried to regain his breath. Above, the helicopter rose higher, Juliette's figure still visible at the edge. She looked down at him, her grin now fully formed—malicious and chilling.

She let me go. The realization hitting him like a gut punch, shattering every instinct he'd trusted.

He tried to move, but rough hands seized him, yanking him upright. Before he could process what was happening, a black bag was forced over his head, plunging him into darkness.

* * *

The haze of confusion lifted slowly as Derrick's senses kicked back into gear. The space around him felt more like a tomb than a box—cramped, suffocating, and unrelenting. Every inhale drew in stale, metallic air, as if the very oxygen had been sucked dry. His knees jammed into his chest, his arms pinned so tightly to his sides that even the thought of movement was exhausting. The edges of the container pressed into him like iron restraints, mocking any attempt at freedom.

He shifted... or tried to... his shoulders meeting unyielding walls. The cuffs dug sharply into his back, adding another layer to the ache spreading through his body. Beneath him, the faint rumble of an engine vibrated through the box, each jarring bump signaling a rough, uneven road. They were moving, but where? His brain clung to every detail like a lifeline.

Voices filtered through the metal walls, muffled and distant, but unmistakably Russian. The sound drifted through the box in short bursts, punctuated by laughter or sharp commands. Whoever they were, they didn't seem concerned about being overheard.

His pulse quickened, the familiar grip of panic clawing at the edges of his mind. He squeezed his eyes shut and pressed his head back against the cold surface behind him. "SERE school," he whispered under his breath. "You've been here before. This is just another exercise. You know the drill."

But this wasn't training. The walls felt closer, the air thinner. In SERE, there was always an end, always a limit to how far they could push you. Out here, there were no rules, no instructors waiting to call it off. His body trembled as claustrophobia inched closer, threatening to overwhelm him.

Breathe.

Lydia's face surfaced in his mind, softening the panic just enough to give him a shred of focus. Her laugh, her smile, the way she always anchored him no matter how chaotic the world got. He held onto her image like a buoy, letting her presence calm the storm inside him. It had worked in training; it had to work now.

But another face barged into his thoughts, shattering the fragile calm. Juliette. The grin she'd worn as she let go of his hand flashed behind his closed eyes, her betrayal replaying like a cruel highlight reel. His chest tightened, anger replacing fear in an instant.

"She did this," Derrick muttered hoarsely, his voice rough in the suffocating space. The ache in his gut twisted into fury, a white-hot flame burning away the helplessness. He wouldn't let it end like this. Juliette had taken everything—his trust, his footing, his safety—and thrown it away. But she hadn't won... yet.

Then he remembered—The alert device hidden in his fake pinky. A surge of hope cut through the despair. It was a long shot, but if he could activate it, maybe—just maybe—it would transmit a signal.

Gritting his teeth, he pushed through the pain and awkwardness of his confined position. Seven quick squeezes. Pain flared in his fingers as the tiny movements scraped the edges of his raw nerves, but he didn't stop. He didn't care. All that mattered was getting the signal out.

Closing his eyes, he prayed the device would find enough range to transmit. *Come on... please work*.

Time dragged by, each second feeling like an eternity. His pulse quickened with every bump in the road, his mind racing through all the possible outcomes.

The hope of rescue mingled with the fear of being trapped here indefinitely, and the gnawing uncertainty clawed at him.

"Someone will find me," he whispered, but even to his own ears, his voice was laced with doubt. "They have to."

Lydia's face came back, stronger this time. She'd know something was wrong. Tae would track it. They had to. But the doubt crept in just as quickly. What if the device didn't work? What if the signal didn't reach?

Worry wouldn't save him, and panic was a dead end. Richie's voice echoed in his mind like it was just yesterday: "Fight like you're the third monkey on the ramp to Noah's ark... and brother, it's starting to rain." The words settled over him, a grim mantra. Waiting was all he could do now—but when the moment came, he'd fight like hell.

CHAPTER 15

The truck rumbled to a stop, and Derrick braced himself, his senses on high alert in the cramped confines of the box. The entire crate shifted as it was lifted off the vehicle, each movement jarring his already aching body. The wooden walls groaned under the strain as he was bounced around inside, his head knocking against the sides with every heavy step of the men carrying him. Finally, the box was dropped unceremoniously to the ground, the impact rattling his bones and leaving him sprawled awkwardly within.

A flood of light blinded him as the lid was ripped open. Squinting, Derrick peered up at the faces looming above—Russian guards with stern expressions, their eyes scanning him for signs of defeat.

But instead of groaning or pleading, Derrick grinned. "Just five more minutes, Mom," he muttered, his voice dry with sarcasm.

The humor didn't land. Rough hands yanked him out of the box, dragging him across a grimy, damp floor. Derrick's feet barely skimmed the ground as they hauled him into a cold, dimly lit room. The concrete walls were cracked. Moisture seeped down their surface causing the air to be damp and stale. With a heave, they threw him to the ground, his body hitting the wet floor with a painful thud.

Derrick groaned, not from the impact but from the thirst clawing at his throat. Still, he couldn't resist. As the guards turned to leave, he called after them, "Careful now! Your Yelp review is plummeting."

One of the guards froze, his expression darkening as he turned back. The massive man loomed over him, his shadow stretching ominously. Derrick, still sprawled on the ground, tilted his head up with a smirk. "Gargantuan," he quipped, sizing the man up.

The giant of a man scowled, his lips curling into a snarl as he delivered a swift kick to Derrick's side, knocking the breath from him and sending pain ripping through his ribs.

Gasping, Derrick curled slightly, his voice strained but defiant. "My bad," he wheezed. "Thought you were someone... nicer."

The guards left, slamming the metal door behind them. Their heavy footsteps echoed down the corridor, leaving Derrick in silence. The cold seeped into his skin, and the metallic taste of the wet floor clung to his tongue as he lapped up what little moisture he could find. It was disgusting, but his parched throat demanded relief.

His body ached, his muscles screaming in protest, but Derrick forced himself to crawl to the wall. Leaning against the cold concrete, he squeezed his finger again, activating the hidden alert device. He knew the signal likely wouldn't penetrate the thick walls, but hope was all he had.

"Well," he thought grimly, "hope's better than nothing."

Hours passed in the freezing darkness. Derrick's thoughts drifted from Lydia's comforting face to Juliette's cold betrayal. Anger simmered beneath his exhaustion, fueling his resolve. He had been trained for this—captivity, interrogation—but training didn't make it any easier. He needed to stay sharp and conserve his strength.

The metal door creaked open, breaking the silence. Derrick squinted as three guards entered, followed by a man who clearly wasn't one of them. Dressed in a perfectly tailored black suit with polished shoes, the man looked out of place against the filthy cell. His sharp eyes gleamed as he stepped closer, a cruel smile tugging at his lips.

"Hello, Mr. Anderson," the man said, his German accent thick but his English precise.

Derrick looked up from the ground, squinting. "Do I know you?"

The man's smile widened, but it carried a chill that made his gut tighten. "No," he replied, his voice dripping with malice. "But I assure you, you will remember me."

One of the guards stepped forward, dragging a large electric battery charger into the room. Derrick's pulse quickened as he watched them plug it in, and his eyes locked onto the jumper cables the guard held in his hand. The cables sparked violently when the guard clapped them together, the crackle of electricity filling the room.

The well-dressed man crouched down, his cold gaze level with Derrick's. "Tell me, Mr. Anderson," he said softly, his tone dangerous, "why are you here?"

Derrick knew this wasn't going to end well, but he had nothing to hide about the basics of his mission. He wasn't here to protect secrets—he was here to find Arabella. So, he took a deep breath and began explaining.

"I'm searching for President Green's daughter. She was kidnapped about a week ago. We tracked her to Kazakhstan, where I met up with an Interpol agent. We followed leads to Kostanay and then to Chelyabinsk. But we had a run-in at the border. I was on my way to Moscow to get new passports when I was betrayed by her."

The man's smile faded, unimpressed. He gave a nod to the guard holding the cables.

Derrick barely had time to brace before the cables touched his wet skin. The shock was instant, his muscles seizing as white-hot electricity ripped through him. He let out a strangled yell, his body writhing in agony.

The cables were pulled away, and Derrick collapsed, gasping for air, his body convulsing from the aftershocks of the electric current. He could feel his heart racing in his chest, his mind reeling as the world around him blurred.

The well-dressed man leaned in closer, his voice a cruel whisper. "Now, Mr. Anderson... let's try this again. Why are you really here?"

Derrick coughed, blood pooling in his mouth from where he'd bitten his tongue. He closed his eyes for a second, trying to center himself through the agony.

The man in the sharp black suit stood over him, impatience clear in his eyes. He demanded answers again, his voice cold and clipped. "Who are you, Mr. Anderson?"

Derrick's mind raced, caught somewhere between pain and the absurdity of the situation. He was too exhausted to think straight, and before he could stop himself, the words tumbled out of his mouth. "I'm a freakin' Tickle Me Elmo..." He stopped abruptly. The irony struck him like a hammer—*Elmo*, the nickname Obadiah had used to taunt him in the past. It was a bitter reminder of how deeply betrayal could cut.

But there was no time to dwell on it. The guard, taking Derrick's sarcasm as defiance, hit him with another surge of electricity. This time the voltage was higher, the shock far more brutal. Derrick's body convulsed violently as the current ripped through him, his mind blanking out in a searing flash of pain. Every muscle screamed as if being torn apart, and his vision exploded in white-hot light.

When it finally stopped, Derrick collapsed again, shaking uncontrollably. Through the haze of agony, he rasped, "Big guy's not a fan of jokes, I see."

The well-dressed man crouched down beside him again, his voice dripping with malice. "Ready to tell me why you're here?" he repeated, his patience clearly running out.

Derrick growled through gritted teeth. "I told you! I'm looking for the President's daughter!"

The man's eyes narrowed, his lips curling into a cruel smile. He stood up straight, mocking Derrick with an almost casual tone. "And why," he asked with a sneer, "would the President of the United States send someone like you for such an important task?"

Derrick's body ached, and his mind was clouded, but this question hit him hard. He couldn't fight the truth, not in this moment. He answered honestly, his voice hoarse. "Because we're friends."

The man raised an eyebrow, clearly skeptical. "Friends?" he repeated, as if the concept was absurd. His smirk faded as he stared down at Derrick, still unsure whether to believe him or not. After a long, uncomfortable silence, the man nodded to the guards and then turned on his heel, leaving the room without another word.

The metal door slammed shut, echoing in the small concrete room.

Derrick wiped his mouth, his breath coming in shallow gasps. He chuckled softly, though it hurt to do so. "That's going to come back and haunt me," he whispered to himself, slumping against the wall, his back still pressed against the cold concrete. He squeezed his pinky again, even knowing that the odds of his signal getting out were slim to none.

The hours dragged on, though Derrick had no concept of time anymore. Sleep eluded him entirely, though not for lack of exhaustion. Every time his body threatened to shut down, the blaring noise would start—sharp bursts of sound piped through unseen speakers. Sometimes it was the shriek of metal grinding against metal; other times, it was ear-piercing static that rattled his skull. The pattern was erratic, designed to keep him on edge, ensuring he never settled into any kind of rhythm.

Between the noise came the cold. The air grew steadily frigid as the damp walls radiated their chill that seeped into his bones. His wet clothes clung to him like a second skin, amplifying the icy bite. Derrick's hands and feet were numb, his breaths shallow as clouds of vapor hung in the air. It was a calculated kind of cruelty—deprive him of sleep, strip him of warmth, and let his own body wage a losing battle against itself.

He curled tighter against the wall, his mind slipping into fragments. *This is just SERE training all over again,* he told himself for the hundredth time as he rocked back and forth to try and generate some warmth.

The door screeched open again, and Derrick flinched involuntarily. A guard stepped in, carrying a bucket filled to the brim with ice-cold water. Without a word, he dumped its contents over Derrick's head, the shock forcing a strangled gasp from his lips as the freezing water coursed down his body, tightening his muscles and stealing what little warmth he had left.

"Stay awake, Mr. Anderson," the guard sneered before stepping back out, leaving the bucket behind as a taunt.

Derrick shivered uncontrollably, his teeth clattering together with such force that a sudden, sharp crack shot through his jaw. The pain was immediate and excruciating, radiating up into his skull and down his neck like a jagged lightning bolt. He froze for a moment, the searing ache overpowering even the biting cold that had consumed him. A metallic tang filled his mouth as blood seeped from the cracked tooth, the sharp edges grinding against his tongue with every shudder of his body.

He groaned softly, but there was no escape from the relentless agony. Every pulse of his heart seemed to thrum against the exposed nerve; each beat a fresh wave of torment. Derrick clenched his jaw reflexively, only to feel the shards of the tooth shift and stab deeper. He wanted to spit, to rid himself of the coppery taste and sharp fragments, but the frigid air made even opening his mouth a challenge.

He whispered the same phrase to himself over and over, a cadence to steady his mind: *Endure. Survive. Fight when the chance comes.*

CHAPTER 16

The dank, frigid air of the cell seeped into Derrick's already battered body as he sat on the floor contemplating his next move. His eyes darted to the light fixture mounted on the wall, its rusted screws barely holding it in place. An idea began to take shape.

Using what strength he had left, Derrick shuffled to the wall and reached up, yanking the light loose with a sharp metallic screech. The wires behind it were long, tangled, and, most importantly, intact. Pulling them free, he twisted them into a long, rope.

Once he had enough length, Derrick quietly dragged himself toward the door. He secured one end of the wire to the door hinge and then pulled the rest to the other side, making sure the door would clear the wire when opened.

Crouching in the shadows, he waited. *Those guards have to be back any second now.*

He could hear footsteps in the hallway, growing louder with each step.

The door creaked open, and the first guard stepped inside. As his boot caught the wire, Derrick yanked it taut causing the guard to stumble. He hit the floor hard, his weapon falling from its holster.

Derrick made a split-second decision he'd come to regret. Instead of reaching for the gun, he looped the chain of his cuffs around the guard's neck. The man thrashed, clawing desperately at Derrick's arms as they struggled on the ground.

The victory was short-lived. The cell door slammed open, and two guards stormed in, their faces filled with fury. One grabbed Derrick and yanked him off, hurling him across the room like a ragdoll. He hit the concrete wall with a bone-jarring impact. Even with the wind knocked out of him and pain radiating through his body, he gritted his teeth and pushed himself back onto his feet.

Before the guards could close in, Derrick charged. He barreled into the second guard, knocking him to the floor. The man's head smacked against the concrete with a dull thud, and Derrick scrambled to grab his weapon, but the third guard was already on him.

Being attacked from behind, Derrick's arms were pinned to his sides. He thrashed violently, kicking and twisting, but the guard's grip was unrelenting. Catching a glimpse of the open cell door, Derrick made a split-second decision. He slammed his head backward, the back of his skull connecting with the guard's face. There was a sickening crunch, followed by a bellow of pain as the man's grip faltered.

Stumbling free, Derrick could see freedom before him. He took one step toward the door when a searing pain stabbed into his thigh. He looked down, his vision swimming, and saw the syringe buried deep in his leg. The liquid inside disappeared as the plunger was pressed.

"Ha! I'm still standing!" he proclaimed proudly, continuing toward the door. But then, his legs wobbled. The room spun, and his vision doubled... then tripled. "Or maybe not," Derrick slurred as his knees buckled. He hit the ground hard as the concrete rose up to meet his face.

***

As the guards dragged him into another concrete room, Derrick's boots scuffed against the cold floor while he struggled to find his footing. The familiar chill in the air wrapped around him, and his eyes swept over the space—a metal table bolted to the floor, a single chair placed ominously at its center. "Déjà vu," he muttered under his breath, his voice dry despite the ache in his throat.

They forced him into the chair, replacing his cuffs with thick leather straps that bound him securely in place. His wrists throbbed where the metal had dug in, but he refused to flinch, fixating on his captors with a deadpan stare.

The door clicked open, and the well-dressed man reappeared, his polished shoes clicking in an unsettling rhythm as he circled the table like a predator sizing up its prey. "Let's try this again, Mr. Anderson. Why are you here in Russia? Who sent you?"

Derrick's eyes narrowed as a thought pierced through the haze of exhaustion. He leaned forward as far as the restraints would allow, his voice sharpening. "If we are in Russia, why do you have a German accent... and how do you know my name?" The challenge hung in the air, his words carrying more strength than his battered body could make good on.

The well-dressed man grinned. An unsettling glimmer of amusement flashed in his expression. "Very good, Mr. Anderson."

Derrick tensed, his body instinctively bracing. "You're not FSB, are you?"

The man's polished smile grew colder. "No, I am not. I *fell from the night*."

Derrick's mouth dropped in disbelief as his voice cracked. "Nightfall? How?"

But the man offered no answers, only a grin that sent a chill through Derrick's already battered frame. The shadows seemed to stretch toward him, as if even the room was complicit in this revelation. His heart pounded against his ribs as he wrestled with the implications.

The guards seized Derrick's head, forcing it back as Derrick clamped his jaw shut. Bitter, acrid liquid spilled over his lips as they tipped a bottle against his mouth after clamping his nose closed. Derrick fought them with every ounce of strength left, spitting and thrashing against the straps, but his lungs betrayed him.

When his air ran out, his mouth opened on instinct, and the liquid burned its way down his throat.

A sickly heat spread through his chest, his stomach twisting in protest as the fog began to settle over his mind. *Scopolamine*. Derrick didn't need to hear them name it to know what it was—the tight grip unfurling in his thoughts, distorting his perception, was unmistakable.

The man leaned in, his voice a cruel whisper. "What do you see?"

For a moment, the room warped, the shadows bending in ways that didn't make sense. Derrick blinked hard, his teeth gritted as he fought to anchor himself in reality. A slow smirk curled his lips, even as the fog thickened. "I see your mother," he rasped with defiance. "And she's disappointed in you."

The man chuckled. "Amusing," he said humorlessly, his tone carrying a hint of dark satisfaction. "But it won't last. Just wait."

The sensation began subtly at first—a faint crawling feeling beneath his skin that sent a shiver racing down Derrick's spine. He shifted uncomfortably, the ache in his wrists momentarily forgotten as the feeling intensified, prickling down his arms and legs like tiny needles. Then he felt it—a soft tickle brushing against his ankle. It came again, closer this time. His gaze dropped to the floor.

A thin, black snake slithered across the concrete, its forked tongue flicking in and out. Another twisted across his boot, circling briefly before slipping under his pant leg, its cold, slick body pressing against his skin. And then another. Derrick's heart pounded in his chest, each beat magnifying the sensation of their scales, their writhing bodies coiling around his ankles and calves.

His throat tightened as he watched the floor come alive. Snakes of all sizes poured in from every corner, slithering toward him in a dark, hissing mass. Their forked tongues darted hungrily at the air, their bodies undulating in a chaotic tide. Derrick instinctively pulled his legs up, thrashing in vain to shake them off.

The first snake slid higher up his boot, slipping beneath his pant cuff and curling against his calf. Its body tightened and released as it climbed, inch by inch. Another snake wriggled beneath his shirt, slithering over his stomach and coiling around his ribs, its slick scales dragging against his skin. The sensation was relentless, unhurried, each movement a fresh wave of dread.

"Stop it... stop it..." he rasped, his voice hoarse and barely audible. But the snakes didn't stop.

The first bite came like a lightning strike, sharp fangs piercing his thigh. Derrick sucked in a shaky breath as venom burned through his bloodstream, spreading like wildfire. Another bite landed higher, then another, each one searing his flesh and sending jolts of pain through his body.

A cold, slimy sensation brushed against his cheek, its presence so unnervingly delicate that for a moment, he wondered if it was his imagination. But then it came again, unmistakably real. He froze, his breath caught in his throat as he felt the forked tongue flicker against his jawline. The snake lingered there, its cold, muscular body pressing against his face, each subtle shift a maddening reminder of his helplessness.

It slid closer, its smooth scales grazing the corner of his mouth. Derrick clenched his teeth, his stomach twisting as the snake's tongue darted out again, the forked tips brushing over his lips. A strangled noise escaped him, somewhere between a gasp and a whimper. He tried to turn his head, but the restraints held firm, leaving him unable to escape the invasive sensation.

The snake seemed to sense his fear, pausing just below his nose as if savoring his dread. Its tongue flicked out again, this time sliding along the edge of his nostril, leaving a trail of cold, wet saliva in its wake. Derrick squeezed his eyes shut, his mind screaming at the encounter as the metallic scent of scales filled his nostrils. Its hissing grew louder in his ears, a cruel symphony of his torment.

Then it moved. Slowly, methodically, the snake coiled higher, its slick body pressing against his temple and curling around his head. Derrick's breath came in shallow, ragged bursts as he felt its tail dragging across his jaw, winding beneath his chin. The creature's weight pressed on his forehead, its body tightening as it settled atop his skull.

When he dared to open his eyes, he was met with the glint of the snake's unblinking gaze. It stared at him, its eyes black and bottomless, a void that reflected his own terror. Derrick's chest heaved as panic clawed at his throat, his body trembling uncontrollably. The snake's head tilted, and for one horrific moment, its tongue darted out, brushing against his eyelid with a feather-light touch. The sensation was like ice and fire all at once, a violation so personal it made his skin crawl and his stomach churn.

"No," he whispered hoarsely, his voice barely audible. "No, no, no..."

The snake didn't care. It slithered down, dragging its scales over his now closed eyes, the faint rasp of its movement like nails on a chalkboard. Derrick wanted to scream, to thrash, to do anything to get it off him, but his body refused to obey. The creature moved with a sinister grace, slipping down his cheek and over his ear, its forked tongue flicking against his earlobe before it slid onto his neck. The faintest pressure of its body against his pulse sent a fresh wave of horror through him.

As it coiled around his throat, Derrick's breathing turned shallow and rapid. The snake tightened slightly, not enough to choke him, but enough to remind him it could. Its head hovered just above his shoulder, and for a moment, Derrick felt the sharp tips of its fangs graze his skin. His entire body shuddered as the creature continued its deliberate, torturous exploration, every movement designed to draw out his terror.

Then, through the turmoil, he saw her. In the center of the commotion, a figure appeared, watching him with wide, innocent eyes.

"Ava..." Derrick's voice cracked, his mind reeling. She looked exactly as he remembered—vibrant, untouched by the horrors of his world. But her gaze carried something unfamiliar. Accusation.

"Why did you let me die?" Her voice was soft, but it cut through his soul like a knife.

"No..." His words trembled, his throat constricting. "I didn't... I couldn't..."

Her expression shifted. The innocence dissolved as her skin paled and stretched tight over fragile bones. Bruises darkened her face, her eyes hollowed and bloodshot. She wasn't Ava anymore, but a shattered remnant of the child he had failed to save, broken and mangled from the storm debris.

A massive snake slithered toward her, its black coils twisting as it approached. It wrapped around her legs, tightening as it climbed. Derrick thrashed in his chair, his restraints cutting into his wrists as he struggled to reach her.

"Ava, no! Run!" he shouted, his voice breaking with desperation.

She didn't move. Her lifeless eyes stared into his, her hand reaching toward him in a silent plea. The snake reared back, its jaws unhinging to an impossible width.

"No!" Derrick roared, straining so hard against the chair that pain lanced through his shoulders.

The snake struck. Its jaws engulfed her feet, then her legs, its body bulging as it swallowed her inch by inch. Derrick screamed her name, his voice raw and hoarse. Ava's gaze never left his, even as the serpent consumed her. Her outstretched hand was the last to disappear, her fingers vanishing behind glistening fangs as the snake's jaws snapped shut.

The silence that followed was deafening. Derrick sagged against the restraints, his body trembling, his breaths ragged. The hissing faded, the snakes retreating back into the darkness.

But Ava's empty stare remained, burned into his mind like a brand.

The room seemed to twist and fold in on itself, his vision swimming with a dark haze that distorted every shadow. A sudden snap echoed in his ears, followed by the crackling roar of flames. Derrick's head whipped to the left, his pulse surging as a blazing inferno erupted in the corner. An oppressive heat surged through the room, and there, in the heart of the fire, stood Emily.

Her silhouette danced in the flames. Her body blackened and contorted as the fire ravaged her flesh. Her once-bright eyes were wide with terror, locked onto his as if pleading for salvation. "Help me, Derrick!" she screamed, her voice raw and broken, cutting through the chaos like a blade.

Derrick's throat tightened as he struggled against his restraints. "Emily!" he shouted, his voice hoarse with desperation. But the flames only grew, swallowing her piece by piece, her skin peeling and cracking, revealing blistered tissue beneath.

The acrid stench of burning flesh filled his nostrils, so thick and putrid that his stomach soured. His chest heaved violently as the sensation overwhelmed him, but there was nothing to expel. His stomach was empty, leaving him dry heaving, each retch tearing at his throat and ribs.

Heat pressed against his face, a suffocating wave that seared his skin as if he were burning alongside her. He looked down at his hands and froze. His flesh bubbled and blistered, twisting into grotesque shapes. Bones snapped beneath the surface, their sharp edges threatening to pierce through. Pain exploded in every nerve, his hands becoming unrecognizable, charred remnants of what they had been.

"Why didn't you save me?" Emily's voice rang out again, louder this time, a shrill accusation that cut straight to his heart. The flames wrapped around her like a living entity, licking up her arms, devouring her hair, leaving nothing but ash in its wake. She writhed in agony, her body convulsing as her screams turned guttural, raw.

Derrick's eyes darted wildly, searching for anything—a way to stop it, a way to wake up. But the fire was everywhere now, consuming the walls, the ceiling, the floor. The room became an inferno, a chaotic swirl of fire and shadow. His vision blurred as faces emerged in the flames, grotesque specters of those he had lost.

The snakes returned, slithering through the fire, their charred scales hissing as they crawled closer. Then came Arabella, her face gaunt and hollow, staring at him with lifeless eyes. "You failed me," she whispered.

Figures pressed closer—Emily, Arabella, Obadiah, even Lydia, and Madeline. Their faces twisted into eerie parodies, their eyes empty sockets that bore into him. Lydia's lips curled back into a silent scream, her arms reaching for him with skeletal fingers, pulling at his resolve, his sanity. Madeline's tiny hands clutched at his wrists, her voice a ghostly wail. "Daddy, why didn't you protect me?"

"No!" Derrick thrashed violently, his voice breaking as he fought against the restraints. Pain tore through his limbs, but he didn't stop. "This isn't real! It's not real!"

But the flames climbed higher, their oppressive heat consuming him, their accusations dragging him deeper into a nightmare he couldn't escape. Every scream, every face, every voice he had ever failed or feared loomed over him, suffocating him in their firelit judgment.

The world around him began to fade, every flicker of light swallowed by the horror in his mind. His body tensed as his senses broke down all at once under the weight of it all.

Derrick's body spasmed violently, his muscles seizing as though an invisible vice had clamped down on him. The world fragmented into sharp flashes of light before plunging him into suffocating darkness. His jaw clenched so tightly that several more of his teeth shattered. Foam bubbled at the corners of his mouth. Thrashing against the restraints, his head snapped back and forth uncontrollably, his body jerking with relentless, brutal force.

"Get the antidote!" a voice barked in Russian, somewhere in the distance.

The room erupted in frantic motion, the sound of footsteps and urgent shouting blending into a dissonant blur. Derrick's awareness flickered, the cold sting of hands fumbling at his face barely registering. His jaw remained locked, defying their attempts to pry it open. Each convulsion ripped through him, shredding what little connection he had to the present.

"He's going to die if we don't get this in him!" another voice shouted, panic riding every syllable.

Somewhere, the metallic clatter of instruments hit the floor, the chaos spinning wildly beyond Derrick's grasp. His body slammed against the chair as another violent spasm tore through him, every muscle screaming in agony. His lungs burned, gasping for air that wouldn't come. The room swirled into a vortex of sound and shadow, pulling him deeper into the abyss.

And then, just as suddenly, it stopped. The seizure released its iron grip, leaving him limp and gasping, his chest rising and falling in jagged, desperate heaves. Every nerve felt raw, his body a hollow shell of exhaustion. Consciousness slipped further away, the distant voices fading into a muffled hum.

Darkness consumed him, pulling him into its cold embrace. The terror that had gripped him moments before gave way to an eerie, hollow void—a silence so deep it felt like the world itself had vanished.

CHAPTER 17

Derrick woke to a searing pain in his head, his body twitching uncontrollably as the aftershocks of the seizure rippled through him. His vision blurred, and every nerve seemed to burn. His limbs were stiff, and the cold concrete floor beneath him felt impossibly hard. He tried to sit up, but his arms refused to cooperate, the effort draining what little energy he had left.

The world slowly came into focus. The dim light overhead flickered, casting jagged, shifting shadows that messed with his mind. He glanced toward the small, grimy window, but it was useless—there was nothing but darkness beyond it, as if the window were just for show. There was no telling what time of day it was anymore. Time had lost meaning in this place.

His heart raced as the memories surged back: the interrogation, the electricity, the torture—it all crashed into him like a wave, and his chest tightened, torn between fear and anger. He didn't know how much more he could take, but he had no choice. He had to keep going. He had to find Arabella. He had to survive.

The heavy metal door groaned open, slicing through the suffocating silence like a blade. Boots thudded against the floor, each step echoing in Derrick's skull. The well-dressed man followed behind, his polished shoes clicking with a maddening calm. Derrick recoiled instinctively, slumping into the corner as though the concrete walls might shield him. His breaths came in shallow gasps, his hands trembling with exhaustion.

The man crouched, his expression a mask of smug satisfaction. "Mr. Anderson," he began smoothly, "you've been a thorn in Nightfall's side for far too long. But all things, even nuisances, must come to an end."

Derrick clenched his jaw, his mind scrambling for something—anything—to stall for time. His lips moved before his brain caught up. "Yeah? What's next, monologuing about world domination?"

The man chuckled, amused by the defiance. "If only you knew the plans you've disrupted. No matter. You won't be around to ruin any more of them."

The words sank like a stone in Derrick's chest. *This is it. They're done toying with me.* He pushed himself upright, body trembling beneath him. "You're making a mistake," he said, his voice steadier than he felt. "Kill me, and the President will scorch the earth to find you."

The man's grin widened. "Oh, we're counting on it."

A single nod from the well-dressed man set the guards into motion. They yanked Derrick to his feet, their iron grips digging into his arms. He thrashed against them, his muscles screaming in protest, but his body was too battered, too drained. They pinned him down with ease, his cheek pressed against the cold concrete.

A sharp sting pierced his neck, cold and burning all at once as the sedative flooded his veins. The room blurred, tilting and spinning as the drug took hold. Derrick's last glimpse was the man's smug face hovering above him, his voice a low murmur. "Goodbye, Mr. Anderson."

The world folded into darkness.

When Derrick woke, the darkness around him was different—more expansive, more ominous. The box he was confined to was larger than before, enough for his legs to stretch out, though his wrists and ankles remained tightly bound. The cuffs bit into his skin with every movement. He shifted slightly, his body screaming in protest from the accumulated torment. *How much time has passed? Hours? Days?*

The box jolted violently, throwing him against the sides. His heart thundered in his chest as it was hoisted into the air. A heavy *thud* rattled through the space as the box was dropped onto a hard surface. Panic clawed at him. "Hey!" he shouted, his voice hoarse. "There's still a person in here!"

A voice responded from outside the box, chillingly familiar—the well-dressed man. "Good," he said, his tone unnervingly calm, almost pleased. "We wanted you awake for this. Go ahead, men."

He listened as the sound of a heavy metal door creaked open, followed by a mechanical clank. A faint yellow glow began to seep through the cracks of the box at his feet.

The conveyor belt beneath him lurched forward, carrying the box toward the yellow glow ahead.

Derrick groaned, "Ugh, what fresh hell is this?"

His breaths quickened as the faint warmth at his feet grew hotter, and the crackling sound of fire reached his ears. The sharp, suffocating scent of burning air filled the space around him. The yellow glow grew brighter, the heat intensifying with every second. Pain shot through Derrick's chest as the full horror sank in.

A crematorium. They're putting me into the furnace!

"No!" he shouted, thrashing against the cuffs. "No, no, no!"

As the box jolted forward, the well-dressed man's voice echoed faintly through the roaring flames ahead. "Do you know why we chose this for you, Mr. Anderson?" His tone was unnervingly casual, like he was discussing the weather. "It's not just about killing you. Death would be far too easy—far too quick. No, this is about erasing you. No grave, no remains, nothing for anyone to find. You'll be a ghost story at best, a name whispered by those too scared to oppose us."

Derrick's breaths quickened as he felt the heat increasing, the reality sinking in. "You won't get away with this," he rasped, his voice hoarse.

The man chuckled, a dark, almost gleeful sound. "Oh, we already have. But you know that, don't you? You've been a thorn in our side from the beginning— Obadiah, Izzy, Deputy Director Caldwell..." He listed the names with a mocking cadence, each one like a nail driven deeper into the moment. "You've ruined plans, killed our people, exposed our leaders. You're a relic of a crumbling agency clinging to outdated ideals, and yet you've been the bane of Nightfall's existence for years."

He leaned closer to the box, his voice dropping to a venomous whisper. "Do you know what I hate most about you, Anderson? You survive. Over and over, you crawl out of the ashes, refusing to stay buried. Not this time. This time, the fire takes you."

The belt lurched forward again, the heat becoming unbearable. Derrick's throat tightened as he fought against the rising panic, his mind flashing to Lydia and Madeline. *This can't be the end. It can't.*

Derrick clenched his jaw, forcing the words through gritted teeth. "It's not over," he growled. "Even if I die, others will take my place. You'll never win."

The man straightened, his smirk widening. "Perhaps. But you won't live to see it."

The box rattled again as the flames roared louder, their suffocating heat licking at the air inside. Derrick pressed his head back against the crate, his fingers twitching toward the hidden device in his pinky. *Please, God. Let it work.* Seven quick squeezes. That's all he could do now.

The well-dressed man's voice carried over the noise one last time. "Goodbye, Mr. Anderson."

CHAPTER 18

A few days earlier in Washington, D.C., the Situation Room was dimly lit. Tae sat alone at the large conference table, his head in his hands as his mind raced. The mission had unraveled before his eyes, and now Derrick—his best friend—was missing. No one had answers. No leads. Just an empty seat where reassurance should have been.

Passing by the door, Lydia paused. Tae's slumped shoulders and distant stare pulled her in. She stepped inside and quietly sat down next to him. Wrapping an arm around his shoulder, she pulled him into a gentle, reassuring hug.

"What's up?" she asked softly, her voice breaking the oppressive silence.

Tae lifted his head, his bloodshot eyes giving him away. He wiped at them quickly, but his expression remained raw. "The train to Moscow arrived a few hours ago," he said, his voice heavy with defeat. "Derrick and Juliette weren't on it."

Lydia's heart sank, a cold dread blooming in her chest. "What do you mean they weren't on it?" she asked, trying to keep her voice steady. "How do you get off a moving train?"

"I don't know," Tae muttered, frustration lacing every word. "There's no trace of them. No reports, no sightings. Nothing." He hesitated, his jaw tightening before he spoke again, his voice lower now. "But there's more."

Lydia leaned in, her heart pounding. "What do you mean 'more'?"

Tae's eyes met hers, his expression grim. "We found Juliette's body."

Gasping, Lydia's hand flew to her mouth. "What? Where?"

"In France," Tae said, his voice strained. "She was killed over a week ago."

Lydia stared at him, her mind reeling. "But... she was with Derrick," she said, shaking her head as if denying it would change the truth. "How—?"

"That's the scary part," Tae interrupted, "Whoever's with Derrick, isn't Juliette. It's not my person."

Suddenly, Lydia's phone buzzed. Her heart raced as she snatched it up, the screen lighting up with Derrick's alert app. Her fingers fumbled to open it, trembling as dread coursed through her veins.

She stared at the screen in disbelief before turning it to Tae. "Derrick's beacon is active. He's in..." She squinted at the unfamiliar name on the screen. "Ul...yan...something?"

Tae looked at the screen, processing the information quickly. "Ulyanovsk," he muttered, confusion flashing across his face. "But their train didn't go anywhere near Ulyanovsk. How did he end up there?"

His hands flew across the conference room's controls, pulling up satellite imagery on the large screen. Within moments, a map of Ulyanovsk appeared, and Tae zoomed in on a specific area—a large, ominous concrete building with a tall chimney jutting from the top.

"This has to be it," Tae said. There was no time to waste.

Grabbing the phone on the conference table, he quickly dialed the Director. "Madam Director, we've found Derrick," he said, urgency sharpening his tone. "He's in Ulyanovsk, and his alert beacon is active."

On the other end, the Director let out a heavy sigh. "This isn't going to be easy," she admitted. "I'll start the diplomatic process, but the Russians won't cooperate quickly. It's going to take time."

Tae's jaw tightened as he shook his head. He had already made his decision. "No, ma'am," he said firmly. "I'm not asking for permission. I'm letting you know—I'm wheels up in ten minutes for Russia."

Lydia stood beside him, her expression equally as stubborn. "And I'm coming with you." Her tone left no room for argument.

The steady hum of the plane's engines filled the small cabin, their rhythmic vibration reverberating through the walls. Tae and Lydia sat in tense silence. They were en route to Uralsk, flying under the radar to avoid prying eyes. Landing directly in Russia would have been a political disaster, something the Director had made crystal clear. But Tae had a plan.

Uralsk was close—just outside Russia's border— and its small, quiet airport offered the discretion they needed. Tae had arranged for a Blackhawk helicopter to be waiting upon their arrival. It was risky, but if everything went according to plan, they'd be in and out of Ulyanovsk before anyone even realized they were there. Derrick didn't have time for red tape.

Lydia sat beside Tae, staring out the window, her expression distant, worry etched into every line of her face. The endless sea of clouds outside the plane seemed to mirror the uncertainty of their mission.

Tae glanced over at her, his tone soft as he tried to offer some reassurance. "He's going to be okay," he said, his voice steady but gentle. "Derrick's tough. He'll make it."

At first, she didn't respond. Her lips pressed into a tight line as tears welled in her eyes. When the dam broke, they fell silently, one after another, down her cheeks. She wiped them away quickly, but there was no stopping them.

"Tae..." she whispered, her voice trembling. "I can't do this anymore. These missions—this life—it's tearing him apart. It's tearing us apart."

Her words hit Tae harder than he'd expected, and he stayed quiet, letting her speak.

"He'll never admit it, but these missions are wearing him down. He's not the same tough guy you knew in training anymore." Her tears flowed freely now, her voice trembling with raw emotion. "I've begged him to stop, to come home. To just stay with us. But he won't. He doesn't know how. He doesn't know how to stop fighting."

Tae nodded, his heart heavy with guilt. She wasn't wrong. Derrick had always been the strongest, the most dependable—the one Tae relied on, no matter what. His best officer. His best friend. But it had come at a cost. The endless danger, the relentless pressure— it was breaking him. And in some ways, Tae knew he bore part of the blame. He'd leaned on Derrick too much and asked too much of him for too long.

"I get it," Tae said, his voice low. "This is on me, too. I've pushed him harder than I should have."

Lydia turned to him, her eyes shimmering with tears, her pain evident. "It's not your fault, Tae. Derrick's always felt like he had to carry the world on his shoulders. But it's crushing him."

Tae reached out, placing a reassuring hand on her arm. "I swear to you, we'll bring him home," he said firmly. "And when we do, things are going to change."

Lydia nodded weakly, clinging to his words for comfort, though the worry still gnawed at her. She understood how deeply rooted Derrick's sense of duty ran. It was an integral part of him, part of what she loved about him. But that same sense of duty was tearing him apart.

Just as a fragile calm began to settle between them, Lydia's phone buzzed again. She glanced at it, her face draining of color as she opened the app. Her shoulders shook as a sob escaped her lips.

"Tae..." she choked out, her voice trembling. "He's calling out again. He doesn't think we're coming. Tae, he thinks we've abandoned him."

The weight of her words hit Tae like a gut punch. His heart sank as he hung his head, the enormity of Derrick's despair overwhelming him. Somewhere out there, Derrick believed he'd been forgotten, left to face whatever horrors surrounded him. The thought tore Tae apart.

"Hold on, buddy," he whispered, his voice barely audible. "We're coming. I swear we're coming."

The plane touched down in Uralsk just as the sun broke the horizon, bathing the desolate tarmac in a soft, orange glow. Tae and Lydia wasted no time, rushing toward the Blackhawk waiting for them at the edge of the airstrip. The crew had been briefed and prepared for the mission ahead.

Lydia's phone buzzed again, the now-familiar notification of Derrick's alert beacon flashing on her screen. Each vibration felt like a knife twisting deeper into her heart, a relentless reminder that Derrick was still out there, still calling for help. She glanced at Tae, her expression desperate, her voice trembling. "It hasn't moved... He's still in the same spot."

Tae nodded. "Then we don't have time to lose. You ready?"

Lydia didn't hesitate. "Let's get him."

As they boarded the Blackhawk, Lydia checked her gear: the rifle's action, the placement of her sidearm, and the snug fit of her ballistic vest. She caught one of the operatives watching her and raised an eyebrow. "What?" she asked, her tone sharper than she intended.

"Nothing," the operative replied, adjusting his own weapon. "You look ready for war."

She didn't respond. She couldn't afford to think about what that meant.

Flying over the barren landscape, Tae kept his eyes sharp, scanning for patrols or signs of enemy activity. The rotor wash kicked up a thick cloud of dust behind them, the ground so close it felt like they could touch it.

"Crossing the border now," the pilot announced over the headset.

The weight of those words settled over everyone aboard. Russian airspace was a hostile threshold, and the consequences of detection were unthinkable. Lydia clenched her jaw as she stared out the window, her knuckles white around the rifle in her lap.

"Russian radar will pick us up if we're too high," Tae said into the comms. "Stay low, stay fast. If they scramble jets, we're done."

Lydia swallowed hard, her voice steady despite the tension in her chest. "If they do, we won't go down quietly." She glanced at Tae, her eyes fierce. "You taught me that."

He smirked faintly, nodding. "Dang straight!"

The pilot banked the helicopter sharply to avoid a cluster of radar towers visible in the distance. Lydia leaned toward the cockpit, studying the terrain ahead. "We've got a blind spot near those hills," she said, pointing to a section of rising ground. "If we hug the slope, we can break their radar line for a few seconds."

The co-pilot turned his head, raising an eyebrow. "You sure about that?"

"Positive," Lydia replied. "We used a similar trick in Baghdad. It'll buy us time."

"Do it," Tae ordered.

The helicopter adjusted its course, skimming so close to the hillside that small rocks and dust kicked up in its wake. Lydia kept her eyes on her watch, counting down. "And... now. Clear."

The Blackhawk shot out of the cover of the hills and back into the open, the city of Ulyanovsk looming in the distance. Tae's pulse quickened as they approached their target: the unremarkable concrete building where Derrick's beacon had been activated.

"This is it," he said, his voice barely audible over the roar of the rotors. "No turning back now."

The Blackhawk descended, its wheels touching down in a barren clearing near the building. Tae, Lydia, and the six operatives aboard moved quickly, leaping out as the helicopter stayed spooled up, prepared for a quick escape.

Weapons at the ready, the team advanced toward the building's entrance, their boots crunching against the frost-covered ground. Guards appeared, shouting orders in Russian, their eyes briefly darting to the U.S. flag on the helicopter as realization dawned. Outnumbered and unprepared, the guards scrambled into defensive positions. Lydia's hands were steady as she aimed and fired, taking down one attempting to flank the team.

"Stay close," Tae told Lydia as they reached the entrance. "We don't know what's waiting for us in there."

She nodded, raising her rifle to the ready position, her heart pounding but her resolve unshaken.

Tae took a deep breath and reached for the handle. The door creaked open, and they slipped inside.

CHAPTER 19

The heat was an unrelenting monster, devouring every inch of the box and searing Derrick's flesh with its fiery breath. His body trembled violently, his muscles spasming as the flames claimed the air around him. The once-sturdy wooden walls were now blackened and brittle, cracking and hissing as the inferno worked its way inward. Small, glowing embers floated in the suffocating space, and the wood above him began to drip fire like molten rain.

He flinched as a drop of flame hit his arm, the searing pain instant and merciless. The smell of his own burning skin clawed at his throat, mingling with the acrid stench of melting rubber as his boots began to fail him. His legs were blistering now, the raw skin tightening and bubbling beneath the relentless assault. The cuffs around his wrists and ankles glowed faintly red, branding him like a condemned animal. The burns were so deep that his nerves had given up screaming— they were silent now, numb to the pain that had once consumed him.

The rubber soles of his boots sagged, softening under the heat. He could feel the blistering ooze beneath them, the sticky, molten mess pressing into his feet. His toes curled instinctively, but there was no escape from the fire's reach. Sweat poured down his face in rivers, stinging his eyes as his body fought to keep him alive in the face of impossible odds.

This is it, Derrick thought, despair washing over him like a tide of molten lead. *The cavalry isn't coming. It all ends here.*

The fire roared louder, drowning out every other sound, its relentless advance consuming the world around him. His mind retreated into itself, shrinking under the weight of guilt and regret. He felt crushed by the enormity of his failures, the mistakes that had led him here.

Emily's face was the first to appear, vivid and raw. Her desperate eyes burned into his mind as if the flames around him had etched her memory into his very soul. He wasn't fast enough. He wasn't good enough. He hadn't saved her... and now he shared her fate.

And then there was the church—the decision that had cost so many lives. He could still hear the screams, feel the debris raining down as the tornado tore through everything. He'd been so sure, so confident in his choice to stay. His confidence killed them.

Juliette's face came next, her betrayal cutting deeper than any burn. She had led him here, her calculated cruelty guiding him to this fiery grave. But it wasn't just her. He had let it happen. He had trusted her. The blame was his alone to carry.

And then, Lydia. Sweet Lydia. Her face rose above the others, radiant and full of love even in the haze of his despair. Madeline's laughter echoed faintly in his ears, a cruel reminder of what he was about to lose. He could see their faces as clearly as if they were standing before him, and the thought of leaving them shattered him in ways the fire never could.

"I don't deserve them," he whispered, his voice cracking under the weight of his anguish. His chest tightened, every breath an agony. "I deserve this... to die alone, in pain."

A tear escaped, rolling down his soot-streaked cheek and sizzling as it met the glowing wood beneath him. He could no longer tell if the heat on his skin was sweat, tears, or the flames themselves.

The fire clawed closer, the box groaning under the pressure. The wood sagged, embers raining down like falling stars, eating away at what little protection he had left. His voice broke as he forced out the words that he thought would be his last, choking on the grief that consumed him.

"I love you, Lydia. I'm sorry for everything. Take good care of Maddie."

The pain now was all-consuming, but Derrick had gone numb to it. He closed his eyes, his lips moving in a silent prayer.

Forgive me. Please, God, take care of them.

The world began to fade as the heat swallowed him whole.

***

The heavy metal doors slammed open as Lydia, Tae, and the team stormed into the building, weapons raised. The heat hit them immediately, suffocating and acrid, the air thick with smoke and the stench of flesh burning.

Gunfire erupted before they could take another step. Men in tactical gear, loyal to the well-dressed man, emerged from the shadows, their weapons blazing. Bullets ricocheted off concrete walls, sparks flying as the sound of gunfire reverberated through the chamber. The team dove for cover, returning fire.

Lydia's heart seized as her eyes locked on the conveyor belt at the center of the room. The box was there, engulfed in flames, edging ever closer to the roaring inferno. *Derrick!* She didn't need to think—she knew.

"No!" she screamed, her voice cutting through the noise.

Ignoring Tae's shouted warning, Lydia ran, weaving through the hail of bullets with reckless abandon. Flames licked at the conveyor belt, the box now glowing red-hot, the wood curling and breaking apart. Every step toward it felt like a lifetime, the heat intensifying with each second. Her boots skidded on the slick floor as she reached it, the fire singing the hair on her arm even from a distance. She could hear Tae yelling her name, but she didn't stop.

Without hesitation, Lydia threw herself against the burning box, shoving it with all her strength. The flames leapt at her arms, biting into her flesh, but she didn't care. The box teetered on the edge before crashing to the floor with a deafening thud, the impact shattering the wood and sending sparks flying.

Behind her, the team pressed forward, cutting down the well-dressed man's guards one by one.

The firefight was over in minutes, the last of the enemy combatants falling to the ground. Silence fell, broken only by the crackle of flames and Lydia's desperate sobs as she worked to free the unconscious figure inside the ruined box.

Tae stepped forward, his weapon trained on the well-dressed man, who stood unarmed but defiant. "You're too late," the man sneered, his voice cold and venomous. "No matter how hard you try, Nightfall will never be stopped."

Tae's scowl grew. That name... he thought they were gone.

The well-dressed man's smirk widened as if daring him. "Pull the trigger," he said mockingly. "It won't change a thing."

Tae's expression didn't waver. A gunshot echoed through the chamber, and the well-dressed man crumpled to the floor, his grin finally gone.

Tae lowered his weapon, inspecting his work. "I'd say that did something. It wiped that stupid smirk off your face, but... it's kind of everywhere now."

***

A loud thud reverberated through the box. At first, Derrick thought the wood was finally succumbing to the flames, collapsing in on him as the fire consumed it. But then the box jerked sideways, pulling him away from the furnace. His mind struggled to keep up, the pain clouding his thoughts. The box teetered on the edge of the conveyor belt before tipping over with a violent crash. He hit the ground hard, the wood splintering and shattering around him.

Flames licked at his clothes, the heat still unbearable as the fire spread across him. He writhed, desperate to extinguish the flames, but before he could move, something heavy slammed onto his chest, pinning him down. A blur of motion—hands beating at the fire, slapping at his burning clothes.

Derrick's vision swam, blurred by smoke and tears. His mind was foggy, the overwhelming heat and pain making it difficult to process what was happening. The fire roared around him, yet someone was there. Someone was saving him.

Who...

His vision cleared just enough to make out a face through the haze. The sight didn't make sense. It almost looked like... Lydia.

But as the figure leaned closer, her tear-filled eyes came into focus. It *was* Lydia.

"Derrick!" she cried, her voice breaking with desperation as she frantically beat at the flames consuming him. "I've got you. Stay with me! You're safe now. I've got you."

The chaos surrounding Derrick blurred as several operatives lifted and carried him from the smoldering wreckage of the furnace room toward the waiting helicopter. His body, ravaged by burns and exhaustion, barely registered the movement, but the overwhelming sense of relief was undeniable. He was out—alive, but just barely. Voices echoed around him, hands gripped him, but it all felt distant, muffled by the haze of pain and adrenaline.

When they reached the helicopter, a medic quickly injected him with morphine. The sharp pain in his legs and arms eased almost immediately, replaced by a dull numbness as the drug took effect. Another team member hooked up an IV of saline and antibiotics, replenishing his dehydrated body and combating the risk of infection. Derrick hardly noticed as his burns were carefully tended to; the roar of the helicopter's blades overhead and the rush of air drowned out everything else as they lifted off from the cold Russian ground.

Lydia was right beside him, refusing to leave his side, her hand resting gently on his shoulder. She kept her eyes locked on his face, fighting back the tears threatening to spill.

Tae was already back in action, sitting near the cockpit, talking rapidly to the pilots back in Ulyanovsk.

"We need to get him to the nearest burn unit," Tae said, his voice strained with urgency. "I'm looking for a friendly city with a hospital that can handle this."

Derrick, groggy from the morphine, overheard Tae's words through the fog clouding his mind. Despite the haze, one thought was crystal clear. "No!" he rasped, his voice weak but insistent. He tried to sit up, but the pain forced him back down. "We have to get to Romania."

Tae didn't respond at first, assuming Derrick wasn't in his right mind, and kept speaking with the pilots. But Derrick wasn't giving up. He reached out, his hand weak but insistent as he grabbed Tae's leg, gripping it as hard as his burnt hands could manage.

"ROMANIA!" Derrick shouted, the desperation clear in his voice.

Tae turned, startled by the outburst, his eyes wide with concern. "Derrick, you're badly injured. We need to get you medical attention. You're not thinking clearly."

"I'm fine," Derrick shot back, his teeth clenched against the lingering pain. The morphine dulled some of it, but his determination was sharper than ever. "I overheard them while I was in the box. Arabella's in Romania—Bran Castle. We have to end this."

Tae's expression tightened, his disbelief flickering for only a moment. "Dracula's Castle?" he asked, the absurdity of the location giving him pause.

But he knew better than to doubt Derrick's instincts when he was this adamant.

"I'll send a team," Tae began, but Derrick shook his head fiercely.

"No!" Derrick's eyes burned with resolve, his breath ragged but forceful. "We need to go now. If we don't, the next time we see Arabella will be on a global broadcast... if you get what I mean."

Tae's jaw tightened as the weight of Derrick's words sank in. Nightfall had Arabella, and was already deep into their endgame. Losing Derrick had likely accelerated their plans. There was no time to waste.

Tae exhaled slowly, his decision made. "Alright, Derrick. We'll go to Romania." Switching coms, he issued the new orders to the pilots. "Change of plans. We're heading to Brașov, Romania. Be ready when we land."

Lydia switched Derrick's headset to a private channel, her voice coming through softly, meant for his ears alone. "Derrick," she began gently, "you're in no condition to keep going. Please, let Tae's team handle this. You've done enough."

Derrick met her gaze, exhaustion etched into his face. But beneath the fatigue, something deeper burned in his eyes—a raw, unshakable determination. Lydia had seen that look before, but never with this intensity. It wasn't just physical pain tearing at him; it was the crushing weight of failure. He had come so close to losing everything—his life, the mission, Arabella.

"I have to," Derrick whispered, his voice hoarse but resolute. "Let me finish this."

Lydia's heart broke as she looked at him. This man—her superhero—was broken, his body barely able to move, and yet, he was still refusing to stop the fight. The determination in his eyes was almost overwhelming. She knew how much this meant to him, but she also knew he wasn't ready for what lay ahead. He couldn't push himself like this, not without consequences.

But she knew Derrick wouldn't listen to words alone. He needed to see for himself that he wasn't ready. She needed to show him the truth, even if it meant hurting him a little.

"Alright," Lydia said softly, her voice challenging. "Let's make a deal."

Derrick raised an eyebrow, confused by her sudden change in tone.

"I'm going to grab your leg," Lydia explained slowly. "Your badly burnt leg. Stop me from doing it."

Derrick's eyes narrowed as he processed her words. It was a test—a way to prove if he still had the strength to fight, to push through the pain. And Derrick wasn't about to fail. Not now.

Lydia's hand slowly moved toward his leg... the leg that had been scorched by the flames in the furnace… the one that was wrapped in bandages and raw from the heat. The mere thought of her touching it sent a jolt of agony through his body, but Derrick steeled himself. He couldn't let her do it. Not without a fight.

Just before her fingers reached his calf, Derrick's hand shot out, his body reacting on instinct. His grip was strong, despite the burns, despite the pain. He caught her wrist, stopping her just before she could touch his injured leg.

Lydia gasped softly, her heart skipping a beat as she looked up at him. Derrick was sitting upright, his eyes locked onto hers, fierce with a determination she had never seen before. His hand, though bandaged and trembling, held hers firmly. His entire body shook with effort, but he didn't waver.

A small smile spread across Lydia's face, her chest tightening with a mixture of pride and sorrow. He was still Derrick—the man who never gave up, the man who defied the impossible. He was still the man she loved.

"Let's go get her," she said, her voice barely above a whisper but brimming with conviction.

CHAPTER 20

As the helicopter skimmed low over the landscape, Tae let out a sigh of relief. Russia faded away behind them, replaced by the relative safety of Kazakhstani airspace.

Moments later, they touched down at the airport in Ulyanovsk. Dust swirled in the rotor wash as the blades slowed, and the team moved quickly to get Derrick transferred to the waiting plane bound for Romania.

But as they were about to move him, he stopped them, determined to walk on his own despite the pain from his burns. Raising his hand, he said, "I've got this." His body screamed in protest, but he wasn't about to let anyone carry him.

Lydia, filled with concern, reached out. "Honey, please," she pleaded softly, her voice full of worry. "Let them help."

Derrick shook his head. "I've only ever needed you," he whispered, extending an arm toward her.

A slight grin tugged at the corners of her mouth, though her eyes glistened with unshed tears. She understood exactly what he meant, and it filled her with a mix of admiration and adoration. Without hesitating, she drew closer, wrapping her arm around his waist.

Tae watched from a short distance following his slow progress. At first, he doubted Derrick could even make it to the plane. His steps were slow and uneven, his body visibly on the brink of collapse. But as they inched closer to the aircraft, something shifted. Derrick's movements became more deliberate, his strides steadier. Each step seemed to draw strength from sheer willpower, propelling him forward despite the pain.

By the time he reached the plane, his walk had almost regained its usual confidence. Lydia's presence had given him strength, but it was Derrick's indomitable spirit that had pushed him through the pain. For the first time that day, Tae felt a flicker of hope.

Maybe we CAN do this, he thought, watching as Derrick straightened himself before boarding the plane. If Derrick could survive what he'd been through and still find the strength to walk, there was a chance. A real chance.

***

As the plane leveled out after takeoff, Derrick leaned back in the cushioned seat, his body sagging with exhaustion. The medic knelt beside him, carefully peeling away the outer layers of his bandages to check his burns. Each movement stung, the raw skin underneath protesting even the lightest touch.

"You're holding up surprisingly well," the medic said, as he replaced the dressing with clean bandages.

"But these pants... they're done for. Let's get you out of them before the smell chokes us all."

Derrick managed a weak smirk. "This is just my signature scent—*Burnt Hero*."

"Tae brought a spare set that he said you could use," Lydia said, pulling out a pair of navy cargo pants, a fresh shirt, and a pair of boots. "Not exactly tailored, but they'll have to do."

Derrick eyed the clothes skeptically. "Tae's spares? I've got a good two inches on him—and that's just in the legs."

"Well," Lydia teased, her lips twitching into a grin, "I think we'll survive seeing your ankles for a few hours. I've always found them rather sexy anyway."

Derrick arched a brow, his lips quirking into a faint smirk. "I'll add that to the list of things I never expected to hear."

With Lydia's help, he eased out of the remnants of his ruined clothes and into the fresh ones. The cargo pants stopped just shy of his ankles, and the shirt clung awkwardly around his shoulders, the sleeves ending a good inch above his wrists. The boots, at least, fit well enough to pass.

Lydia stood back, crossing her arms as she surveyed him with a mix of concern and humor. "Well, if nothing else, you'll be starting a new trend," she quipped. "The too-short, barely-buttoned, battle-scarred look."

Derrick chuckled softly, the sound more of a rumble in his chest. "As long as it doesn't include the smell of burnt leather and rubber, I'll take it."

"Fair point," Lydia said, stepping closer to carefully smooth the shirt over his shoulder. Her fingers lingered for a moment. "Better?"

"Much," he said with a soft smile. "Thanks, Honey."

She gave him a soft grin before kissing him. "Anytime."

***

By the time the plane touched down in Brașov, Derrick felt more alive than he had in days. The morphine and saline had done their job, but his body was far from healed. His legs were still wrapped in bandages and requiring frequent doses of pain medication, but the fire inside him burned brighter than ever. He was ready to end this.

When the plane stopped, there was no time to waste. The group split into two SUVs waiting on the tarmac. Derrick and Lydia climbed into the first vehicle with two officers, while Tae and the remaining three operatives took the second. The convoy moved quickly through the darkened streets, the towering Carpathian Mountains looming in the distance like silent sentinels.

As they neared Bran Castle, the vehicles slowed, their headlights cutting through the dense fog that clung to the ground like a ghostly shroud. The castle's imposing silhouette emerged, its spires piercing the night sky. "This place gives me the creeps," one of the officers muttered, earning a sharp glance from Derrick.

"It should," he said. "It's not just for show. Nightfall doesn't pick locations at random."

The officer frowned. "You're saying this isn't just a hideout?"

"Exactly. The castle isn't just intimidating; it's isolated, defensible, and riddled with tunnels that could hide an army. Perfect for smuggling or staging operations. Nightfall knows what they're doing."

The SUVs pulled off the road, disappearing into the cover of dense trees surrounding the castle grounds. Tae stepped out of the lead vehicle, signaling for everyone to gather.

"We're about a mile out," he began, glancing between Derrick and the rest of the group. "Team One comes with me to the eastern approach. Team Two, Derrick's leading you through the forest to the back entrance. It's a smaller entry point but should get you closer without being spotted."

Entering the castle, the air was thick with dust and the faint scent of mildew. Flashlights swept across ancient stone walls as the team navigated the labyrinthine corridors. The castle seemed to whisper secrets, every creak of the floorboards and distant rustle amplifying the tension.

The fortress, often called Dracula's Castle, was steeped in both history and legend. Built in the 14th century, it had served as a strategic military stronghold, guarding the mountain passes between Transylvania and Wallachia. Nightfall likely chose it not for its gothic allure but for its defensible design—thick stone walls, hidden passages, and a commanding position over the surrounding terrain. It was as much a fortress as a psychological weapon, its dark history unnerving even the most hardened soldiers.

Derrick couldn't ignore the irony. The castle's infamous legends—whispers of bloodthirsty tales surrounding *Vlad the Impaler*, the inspiration for Bram Stoker's *Dracula*—added an extra layer of dread. Even if the connection to Vlad was tenuous, the psychological effect was undeniable. Nightfall didn't just want to hide; they wanted to haunt.

"Stay close," Derrick ordered. Lydia nodded, her eyes scanning every shadow, her rifle drawn and ready.

They pushed open a set of heavy wooden doors inside, revealing a dimly lit hall that stretched into shadowy darkness. Derrick led the way, his footsteps echoing on the cold stone floor as he, Lydia, and the team of operatives stepped inside. Flickering candles mounted on the walls cast long, wavering shadows, making the corridors seem alive with movement.

The group pushed cautiously through the winding passages of the fortress. Narrow stairways twisted unpredictably, leading them both up and down as the flickering candlelight threw eerie shapes across the walls. Every turn felt charged with an unseen presence, the castle's infamous legends weaving through Derrick's thoughts. The oppressive atmosphere gnawed at him with each step.

The deeper they ventured, the more unsettling it became. Derrick caught a glimpse of something—a fleeting figure at the edge of his vision, darting out of sight. His heart pounded as the shadows seemed to close in. The old stories surfaced unbidden in his mind, filling him with the uneasy sense that unseen eyes were following their every move. They passed a suit of armor, and Derrick froze. For a fleeting moment, he swore it moved—a ghostly flicker of something dark and menacing.

His grip on the rifle tightened as he halted abruptly, turning his weapon towards the statue.

Lydia smirked, smacking him lightly on the back of the head. "No more morphine for you," she whispered, her playful tone breaking the tension and snapping him out of his paranoia.

Blinking, Derrick shook his head as they rounded another corner. "I swear, I just saw—"

"Dracula?" Lydia teased quietly, her wry smile softening the tension.

Derrick sighed, conceding with a small shrug. "Yeah, maybe."

As they ventured deeper into the castle's intricate corridors, Derrick's flashlight beam caught movement at the far end of the hall. Three figures stood silhouetted against the faint light streaming through a high window, and Derrick's heart stopped as he recognized the one in the center.

His rifle lowered slightly as disbelief flickered across his face. *Juliette. Here?* The thought barely had time to register before instinct took over. He raised his weapon again and fired two shots. The figures scattered, the bullets striking one of them, who crumpled to the ground. The other two disappeared into the shadows, their footsteps echoing in the distance.

"Move!" Derrick barked, sprinting forward with Tae close behind. Lydia and the officers covered their six, weapons trained on the empty hallway behind them.

They reached the fallen figure, a young man dressed in dark tactical gear. Blood pooled beneath him, staining the ancient stone floor. Tae knelt, checking for weapons while Derrick pressed a hand to the man's chest, trying to stem the bleeding.

"Who are you working for? Where's Arabella?" Derrick demanded, his tone sharp.

The man's lips curled into a weak, mocking smile. Coughing, blood bubbled at the corner of his mouth. "You're too late. Night has come!" he rasped before his eyes glazed over and his body went limp.

Derrick cursed under his breath, clenching his fist before punching the ground. Tae glanced his way, his expression growing grim. "We need to move. They know we're here now."

He nodded and pushed himself to his feet. "Let's go. Stay sharp," he said, as they pressed on deeper into the castle.

The corridor seemed to stretch endlessly as they followed the faint sound of retreating footsteps. Rounding another corner, they spotted Juliette darting behind a large, imposing wooden door at the end of the hall. The team slowed their pace, weapons drawn.

Derrick approached the door, his hand hovering near the handle. He glanced back at the group. "You know, this is a trap, right?" His voice carried a grim certainty.

Lydia stepped up beside him, her gaze fixed on the door. "But if Arabella is in there, we have to."

Tae cracked his knuckles and grinned. "Let's knock on the door. We can try to sell them some cookies. Everyone loves cookies."

Derrick shot him a sidelong glance, eyebrows raised. "Cookies? Did you hit your head getting out of the SUV?"

Tae shrugged, the grin never leaving his face. "Hey, I've got some Thin Mints in my pocket. They're irresistible."

Derrick sighed, grasping the handle of the door. "Uh... you're so weird. Anyway, on my count. One, two..."

CHAPTER 21

The room beyond was dim, lit only by the unsteady glow of candles. Shadows stretched and flickered across the stone walls, but it wasn't the room's eerie ambiance that caught Derrick's attention—it was the camera equipment. Tripods were positioned throughout the space, each holding a video camera pointed at various angles.

One was aimed directly at a small figure tied to a chair against the far wall of the room.

It was her – Arabella.

Her wide eyes brimmed with fear, her pale face stark against the dim light. She looked fragile, terrified, and utterly alone.

"Arabella!" Lydia gasped, slinging her rifle behind her back and rushing forward instinctively.

Before she could take another step, a voice slithered out from the shadows, low and venomous. "Ah, ah... not so fast, my pretty."

***

Thousands of miles away, back in Washington, D.C., the atmosphere in the Situation Room was thick with tension. The President sat at the head of the long table, his face drawn and pale, his eyes fixed on the large screen dominating the room. Katherine sat beside him, her hands clenched tightly in her lap, her knuckles white.

The room was filled with the sounds of phones ringing, advisers scrambling for solutions, and the grim reality of what was unfolding before them.

On the screen, Arabella sat tied to a chair, her face ashen, eyes wide with terror. The cameras shifted angles every few seconds, capturing the haunting scene from multiple perspectives, amplifying the horror.

"We need to shut this down," the President boomed, "Get the network off the air. Now!"

One of the aides seated at the far end of the table shook his head grimly. "Sir, they've bounced the signal across multiple satellites. It's live-streaming, and we can't isolate the feed fast enough."

Katherine's eyes filled with tears as she stared at the screen, her heart breaking with every passing second. "Do something," she whispered, her voice cracking. "Please, do something."

The President gripped her hand tightly, his knuckles matching her own whiteness. They watched Arabella flinch as the cameras shifted again, her terror dissected from every angle, every tear magnified for the world to consume. It was a grotesque invasion... a living nightmare. For the first time in his life, the President felt utterly helpless—just another horrified spectator, paralyzed as his daughter's fear played out like a macabre performance.

***

The sharp sound of a gun being cocked cut through the air, sending a wave of cold dread rippling through the room. Derrick snapped his rifle up, his eyes scanning the shadows.

A tall figure emerged, his polished shoes clicking against the stone floor with each deliberate step. His presence was commanding, his cold, calculating gaze sweeping the room, lingering on each person as if appraising their worth.

"Stay back," the man warned, his voice calm and measured, its tone steeped in authority. A second figure stepped forward, casually waving a pistol at Lydia as if it were a mere accessory.

"Who are you?" Derrick demanded, his rifle trained unwaveringly on the two.

The man's smirk deepened as he clasped his hands behind his back. His voice was smooth, deliberate, and laced with menace. "Names are trivial, Mr. Anderson, but you may call me Cyrus.

Derrick's scowl hardened. Behind him, Tae and the operatives fanned out, scanning for any movement in the shadows. Lydia froze, her gaze flicking between Arabella tied to the chair, and the man with the gun.

Then, beside Cyrus, another figure stepped into the flickering candlelight—Juliette.

Derrick's breath caught, seeing her. The same confident stride, the piercing eyes that had haunted him since the mission in Moscow. But something didn't feel right. There was a coldness to her expression, a sharpness that cut through any familiarity. Lydia glanced at Derrick, her eyes narrowing at his hesitation.

"Juliette," Derrick said, his voice edged with disbelief and anger. His finger retracted slightly on the trigger.

From behind, he heard Tae say. "Derrick, that's not Juliette."

His eyes flicked to Tae and then back to the woman before him. She smirked, tilting her head slightly. "Ah, always the clever one, Tae," she said, her voice dripping with mockery. "No, Derrick, I'm not Juliette. The real Juliette is... well, let's just say she didn't make it out of our ambush in Prague."

Stepping forward, Cyrus's smirk widened. "Allow me to introduce her properly. This is Elena—a loyal and highly effective operative of Nightfall."

Derrick's teeth clenched, his voice cutting through the tension. "You've been impersonating her this whole time."

Elena shrugged, her mocking smile returning. "It was a challenge at first. Juliette was sharp, confident, but so predictable. It wasn't hard to step into her shoes. The real fun came when I got to... experiment. Blend her confidence with Lydia's tenderness. You should've seen your face in Chelyabinsk, Derrick. You didn't know what to think. Imagine my surprise when we... *intertwined* that night."

Lydia's gaze snapped to Derrick, confusion and hurt flickering in her eyes. "What is she talking about?"

The grip on his rifle tightened as he locked eyes with Lydia. "She's lying. It's just another one of their games."

"Oh, come now, Derrick." Elena's smirk widened. "You're not going to tell her about Chelyabinsk? About how I made you question everything? You didn't know whether to trust me or take me out, and it was glorious."

Lydia's eyes narrowed as she shifted her aim toward Elena. "You think I'd believe anything coming from you? You're nothing but a manipulative coward hiding behind a dead woman's face."

Elena's expression faltered, the flicker of annoyance quickly masked by her calmness. "Touché, Mrs. Anderson. But the cracks are already forming. You'll wonder, even if you don't admit it."

"Enough of this. You don't get to rewrite the truth." Derrick growled as he stepped forward, his rifle trained on Elena's chest. "Whatever you're trying to do, it ends now."

Cyrus chuckled, gesturing for Elena to step back. "Elena, your part in this performance is over. You've played it beautifully, but now, Mr. Anderson, it's time for the final act." He spread his arms wide, his smirk returning. "You've walked willingly into our trap."

Derrick's gaze shifted back to Cyrus, his anger simmering just below the surface. "You think you've outplayed me? You've underestimated me."

Pacing slowly, Cyrus's gaze locked onto Derrick. "You know, I wasn't always like this," he began, his tone casual, almost conversational. "Once upon a time, I wore a different suit. Worked for a different cause. Sound familiar?"

Derrick's scowl deepened. "Let me guess. MI6," he said sharply, his tone dripping with disdain.

Cyrus's smirk widened. "Astute as ever, Mr. Anderson. Yes, I was one of Her Majesty's finest—or so they claimed. I gave them years of my life, carried out their dirty work, and cleaned up their messes. I was the best at what I did. Until an op went south. A routine extraction turned into a bloodbath. My team... my friends... gone." He gestured to the side of his face, where faint scars caught the flickering candlelight. "And I was left like this."

Lydia's voice cut through the room, sharp and defiant. "So what? You failed, and they let you go. That's life. But this? This is just you throwing a tantrum."

Cyrus chuckled softly, his tone chilling. "A tantrum? Oh no, Mrs. Anderson. This is far more refined. Do you know what MI6 did when I finally made it back? Did they help me? Stand by me? No. They called me a liability, turned their backs, and discarded me like yesterday's trash. A quiet discharge. A handshake. And that was it."

Derrick's voice was a blade cutting through Cyrus's words. "So, this is revenge? Because they let you go?"

Cyrus's eyes gleamed as he met Derrick's gaze. "Oh, it's far more than revenge. During my exile, I learned something. The world isn't run by governments or intelligence agencies. It's ruled by fear. Control that, and you control everything. That's what Nightfall understands. That's why I joined them."

Derrick took a step forward, his red dot still centered on Cyrus. "And you think terrorizing a girl and her family proves your point? That's not power—it's desperation."

Cyrus's smirk faltered briefly, but he quickly recovered, his tone rising with conviction. "They didn't just give me power—they gave me purpose. And now, I get to return the favor to the people who betrayed me. MI6, the CIA, the entire Western world—they'll all see what happens when you cross someone like me."

"You think this will make you unstoppable?" Derrick asked. "It's just another delusion, Cyrus. Power built on fear always crumbles."

Cyrus laughed, a sharp, hollow sound. "Oh, Derrick, I've studied the game longer than you can imagine. And I know the truth: People don't respect strength. They respect fear. And tonight, the world will learn to fear Nightfall."

He gestured grandly to the cameras positioned throughout the room. "In moments, this broadcast will reach every major network at every corner of the globe. They will see what we are capable of, that no fortress is too impenetrable, no figure too powerful. Not even the President of the United States can protect his own daughter from us."

Lydia's hands clenched into fists at her sides, her eyes blazing with fury. "You're nothing but cowards hiding behind a spectacle," she spat.

Cyrus's eyes gleamed as he turned his attention to her. "Ah, but that's where you're wrong, Mrs. Anderson. Fear is a weapon far more potent than any bullet. By the time this is over, the world will know the reach of Nightfall. Governments will tremble, leaders will fall, and chaos will reign." He gestured toward Arabella, tied and trembling in the chair. "And Arabella Green will be the first casualty of a new era."

Derrick's grip on his rifle tightened, his voice cutting through the tension like a blade. "You won't get away with this."

Cyrus tilted his head, as though amused by the statement. "Oh, but I already have. The cameras are rolling, the message is being delivered, and you, Mr. Anderson, are a mere pawn in my theater."

Derrick's eyes narrowed as Cyrus's words settled over the room. Something felt off. The hairs on the back of his neck stood up.

"You feel that?" Tae asked nervously, raising his rifle towards the shadows in the room.

"Yeah," Derrick replied as his eyes traced the faint grooves in the stone walls—grooves that hadn't been there before.

Tilting his head, Cyrus watched them with amusement, his calm demeanor only amplifying the unease. "Ah, Mr. Anderson, always the sharp one. But I'm afraid you're a little too late."

Before Derrick could respond, the door behind them slammed shut with a deafening crash. A series of metallic clicks echoed through the chamber as hidden panels in the walls slid open. Dozens of armed men poured into the room, their rifles trained on Derrick and his team.

Tae sighed, as the operatives closed ranks around them. "Guess we're doing this the hard way."

CHAPTER 22

Gunfire erupted as bullets ricocheted off the stone walls around them. The team sprang into action. Derrick's first priority—The man beside Cyrus with Lydia in his gunsights. Two quick bursts, and he dropped to the floor.

Seeing this, Lydia dashed for Arabella, ignoring the firefight around her. "It's okay. We're going to get you out of here," she reassured as she quickly untied her restraints.

Derrick fired another controlled burst, dropping a guard attempting to flank their position. The heat from his rifle's barrel burned against his gloves, the weapon heavier in his hands with each shot. His ears rang from the relentless gunfire echoing in the enclosed stone chamber.

"One down, right side still hot!" Tae shouted, ducking as bullets slammed into the pillar beside him, sending chunks of stone flying. He pulled a smoke grenade from his belt, yanking the pin before throwing. "Smoke out!"

The grenade hit the floor with a metallic clink before erupting into a thick gray cloud that quickly spread across the chamber. The guards' gunfire grew erratic as the smoke obscured their line of sight.

"Cover her!" Derrick barked, turning to fire at a guard spraying bullets from behind a toppled column. His shots forced the man to duck, but not before stray rounds slammed into one of the camera rigs, sending plastic chunks flying. Derrick ducked instinctively, cursing as shards peppered his shoulder.

Lydia yanked the last knot free, pulling Arabella's trembling form into her arms. "We're moving!" she shouted.

"Go!" Derrick yelled, laying down suppressive fire as Lydia and Arabella darted toward a column for cover. A sudden groaning sound filled the chamber—a low, ominous creak. Lydia's head snapped up just as one of the ancient stone columns began to tilt.

"It's coming down!" Tae shouted.

"Run!" Lydia grabbed Arabella's hand and sprinted, the girl stumbling behind her. The massive column crashed to the ground, shattering into chunks of stone that skidded across the floor. Lydia yanked Arabella forward, both of them diving to avoid the falling debris. Dust filled the air as the column's impact shook the chamber.

"Keep moving!" Derrick called, firing at a guard trying to advance through the smoke.

Lydia pulled Arabella to her feet, coughing as she climbed over the crumbled remains of the column. Her palms scraped against the rough stone, but she ignored the pain, dragging Arabella with her. Another burst of gunfire forced them to duck behind the next intact column, Lydia throwing her arms around Arabella to shield her.

***

In the Situation Room, Katherine gasped, her hand covering her mouth as she watched the chaos unfold on the screen. Smoke and flashing muzzle fire obscured most of the view, but she caught sight of Lydia shielding Arabella with her body. "They're going to kill her," she whispered, tears streaming down her face.

The President's hand slammed onto the table. "We need to shut this down!" he shouted, though he knew no one in the room had the power to act.

***

Back in the chamber, an operative's sharp cry pierced through the gunfire. "I'm hit!" The man collapsed against the rubble, clutching his leg where blood seeped through his pants. Another operative dragged him back into cover, firing one-handed to keep the guards at bay.

"Tae! Take the left!" Derrick called, his voice hoarse from shouting. Tae ducked low, firing as he maneuvered to a better position. The smoke began to spread further, providing Derrick's team a momentary advantage.

"Lydia, you clear?" Derrick shouted, his voice barely cutting through the chaos.

"Not yet!" Lydia called back, pressing Arabella closer to the column as more bullets zipped past. The ancient stone provided little comfort as fragments chipped away under the relentless assault.

Derrick adjusted his stance, the heat of his rifle making it harder to hold steady. Sweat dripped down his temple as he scanned for the next threat. His ears throbbed from their constant ringing.

"Tae, suppress the right!" Derrick ordered, aiming at another advancing guard. His shots hit their mark, dropping the man mid-step. "Lydia, move now!"

She didn't hesitate. Grabbing Arabella's hand, Lydia pulled the girl along as they darted toward another column, dodging debris and diving for cover as bullets whizzed by. Behind her, Derrick's rifle fired again, keeping the guards pinned down.

But then his rifle clicked empty, the bolt locking back. "Out!" he shouted, ejecting the magazine. Reaching for another, his hand came back empty. A quick glance told him his team was running low, their return fire slowing. Without hesitation, he drew his sidearm and snapped back into action.

"Hold your ground!" Tae shouted, his voice hoarse as he fired another burst. The smoke thickened, obscuring the far end of the chamber, but the guards were thinning out. Those still standing fired wildly, desperation clear in their movements.

"Right flank clear!" one of the operatives called, crouching behind cover as he reloaded.

Derrick pressed forward, staying low as he advanced. He spotted movement through the haze—a guard raising his rifle. Two quick shots from Derrick's pistol dropped him before he could fire. Another figure emerged from the smoke, only to be taken down by Tae's precise burst.

"Derrick!" Lydia's voice called out. He turned to see her still shielding Arabella, her body hunched protectively over the girl.

Then he saw her—Elena. She emerged from the smoke, her eyes locking on Lydia. A smirk spread across her face as she raised a pistol, her target unmistakable.

Without thinking, Derrick moved. "Lydia, get down!" he yelled, throwing himself between her and Elena just as the first shot cracked through the air. The impact drove him backward, the force of the round slamming into his vest. A second shot hit him as he stumbled.

Derrick hit the ground hard, the breath knocked from his lungs. Pain radiated through his chest, but his hand tightened on his pistol. Gritting his teeth, he raised the weapon and fired three rapid shots.

The rounds found their mark, striking Elena in the chest. Staggering, her smirk disappeared as her gun slipped from her grasp. She collapsed to the floor, her body motionless.

***

Katherine's gasp filled the tense silence. "He's been shot!" she cried, her voice trembling. Clutching the edge of the table, her eyes glued to the screen as Derrick collapsed. "Oh my God, he's down!"

The President shot to his feet, his hands gripping the edge of the table so tightly his knuckles turned white. "Get me someone in the field!" he barked at the room of stunned aides. "What's happening? Is he alive?"

"Wait!" one of the aides exclaimed, pointing at the monitor. "He's moving!"

***

Lydia crawled toward him, her hands reaching for him. "Derrick, talk to me."

"I'm... fine," Derrick managed, though his voice was strained. He rolled onto his side, his pistol still raised, scanning for any remaining threats. Tae and the operatives moved quickly, sweeping the chamber and firing the last shots needed to clear it.

"Clear!" Tae called, his voice sharp. The gunfire stopped, leaving only the crackling of distant flames and the rasp of strained breathing.

The room was thick with smoke, the sharp stench of burnt gunpowder filling the air. Spent casings littered the stone floor, and the remnants of the toppled column still smoked faintly from the grenade blast. Derrick's chest throbbed from the impact, each breath a reminder of how close it had been.

Lydia reached him, her hands trembling as she checked his vest. "Derrick, are you sure?"

He pushed himself upright with a groan, wincing at the pain. "Vest stopped it," he said, his voice tight. "Just bruised. Go check on Arabella."

Lydia hesitated, her eyes lingering on him for a moment before she turned back to the girl. Arabella was trembling but unhurt, her wide eyes fixed on Derrick. Lydia pulled her close, whispering softly to calm her.

Tae stepped out of the dissipating smoke, his rifle lowered but his eyes scanning the room. "Clear on this side," he said, glancing toward Elena's motionless body. His gaze swept toward the far end of the chamber, where the heavy steel door Cyrus had entered through now stood ajar. Tae's jaw tightened. "Cyrus is gone."

Derrick followed his gaze, his expression darkening. He forced himself to his feet, ignoring the sharp ache in his chest. "Figures," he growled. "He set this up from the start."

Tae snorted, shaking his head. "So much for not running, you coward," he said, his tone laced with frustration.

Derrick's eyes narrowed as he stared at the open door. "He'll get what's coming to him," he said grimly. "But first, we get Arabella out of here."

Taking a few slow steps toward Elena, Derrick glared at her lifeless body sprawled across the stone floor. Lydia watched, pondering what was going through his mind.

Then, with a sharp kick to her side, he muttered under his breath, "Guess you won't be impersonating anyone else, you crazy—"

"Derrick!" Lydia's voice cut through the haze, sharp with surprise as she instinctively covered Arabella's ears. "Language!"

Derrick blinked, caught off guard. A faint blush crept up his neck as he glanced at her. "What?!? I didn't actually say it!"

Lydia shook her head, though the corners of her mouth twitched upward. "You're unbelievable."

The towering shadow of Bran Castle loomed behind them as the team trudged toward the waiting SUVs. Lydia carried Arabella in her arms, the young girl trembling against her chest. Every few steps, Lydia whispered reassurances, her voice soft and calm, but Arabella's small frame still shook with the aftermath of terror.

As Lydia rounded the side of the lead SUV, she froze. Derrick stood leaning against the vehicle, his posture deceptively casual despite the pain etched across his face. One hand gripped the doorframe for balance, the other rested against his bruised ribs. The faint glow of dawn highlighted the exhaustion in his eyes and his heavier than normal breathing, but there was also a flicker of relief.

"Derrick," Lydia said softly, her voice edged with worry as her eyes caught the slight tremble in his hand.

He quickly shifted, standing straighter and forcing a small smile.

In an attempt to brush off her concern, Derrick shifted his gaze to Arabella, his lips twitching into a faint, reassuring smile. "Looks like we found our princess," he said softly, approaching them.

Arabella peeked out from the blanket draped over her shoulders, her wide eyes locking on Derrick. She said nothing, but her trembling eased ever so slightly at his calm presence.

Tae appeared from the other side of the SUV, carrying his rifle slung casually over his shoulder. He glanced between Derrick, Lydia, and Arabella before smirking. "Well, this is cute," he quipped, leaning against the hood. "Like the end of one of those family reunion movies. Only, y'know, with more explosions and fewer golden retrievers."

Derrick let out a breathy chuckle, shaking his head. "You missed your calling, Buddy. Comedy gold right there."

Tae grinned, undeterred. "I know, right? Maybe I'll start a podcast: 'Rescues, Jokes, and Just a Dash of Heroism.' You can be my first guest."

"Hard pass," Derrick replied, his tone light. "You'd just make me do all the talking."

Lydia shook her head, a small smile breaking through her exhaustion. "You guys are insufferable."

"Fine," Tae said, raising his hands in mock surrender. "But for the record, I'm excellent with golden retrievers."

Arabella's lips twitched, the faintest hint of a smile breaking through her fear. Lydia noticed and pressed a gentle kiss to the top of her head. "Let's get her inside," she said softly, glancing at Derrick.

He nodded, opening the door for them. As Lydia helped Arabella climb into the back seat, Tae gave Derrick a look.

"You okay?" Tae asked, his tone quieter now.

Derrick's hand brushed against his ribs, and gave a slight shrug. "I'll live."

"Good," Tae said with a smirk. "Because I'm not carrying you."

The convoy roared to life, the engines breaking the quiet of the early morning. The SUVs sped down the winding mountain roads as the sun rose steadily over the horizon. It was as if the world itself was waking from the nightmare they had just endured.

Inside the SUV, Derrick pulled out his phone, scrolling through his contacts before hitting send. Habatian answered immediately.

"Mr. President," Derrick said, his voice steady despite the exhaustion. "We've got her. Arabella is safe."

There was silence on the other end as the moment sank in. Then, faintly, Derrick could hear the background of the Situation Room erupting into applause and cheers. The President's voice broke through, thick with emotion. "Thank God! Thank you, Derrick. Thank you."

Derrick allowed himself a small, weary smile. "We're on our way to the airport now. Should be back at Andrews in about six hours."

"We'll be there," the President said firmly. Then, after a pause, he added, "Katherine wants to speak to her."

"Of course," Derrick replied. Turning in his seat, he held the phone out to Lydia. "Katherine wants to talk to Arabella."

Lydia smiled and crouched slightly to hand the phone to the girl. "It's your mom," she said softly.

Arabella hesitated, her wide eyes searching Lydia's face for reassurance. Then, with trembling hands, she took the phone. "Mom?" Her voice was barely above a whisper.

"Arabella," Katherine's voice came through, thick with relief. "Oh, my baby. Are you okay? Are you hurt?"

Tears welled in Arabella's eyes as she gripped the phone tightly. "I'm okay, Mom. I'm okay now, thanks to Lydia." Her voice broke on the last word, and Lydia pulled her closer, wrapping an arm around her.

Katherine's voice wavered, the sound of quiet sobs barely audible through the phone. "I love you so much, Arabella. We're waiting for you. We'll be there as soon as you land."

"I love you too, Mom," Arabella replied, her voice soft but steady.

Lydia gently took the phone back as Arabella leaned against her, the weight of the ordeal catching up with the girl. She handed it to Derrick, who held it to his ear.

"She'll be back in your arms soon," Derrick said to Katherine. "We'll keep her safe."

"I know you will," she replied, her voice steadier now. "Thank you, Derrick. For everything."

Ending the call, Derrick leaned back in his seat, staring out at the rising sun. For the first time since stepping foot in the castle, he allowed himself a moment of quiet. They weren't out of danger yet, but they were heading home.

The SUVs screeched to a halt beside the waiting plane, its engines humming steadily, ready for takeoff. Tae and the operatives formed a loose perimeter, scanning for any threats as Lydia ushered Arabella toward the aircraft.

Derrick brought up the rear, his steps faltering as exhaustion seeped into his body. The adrenaline that had propelled him through the firefight was gone, leaving behind raw, unrelenting pain. His legs burned with every step, the bandages on his burns damp with sweat. His chest ached from the impacts his vest had absorbed, and his vision blurred briefly as his body fought to keep him upright.

"Derrick," Lydia called, as she paused at the base of the plane's steps. Her eyes met his, filled with concern. He managed a faint nod, signaling he was still with them, even if just barely.

Lydia glanced over her shoulder, catching the medic's attention. With a quick nod from her, he closed the distance, syringe in hand.

"What are you—?" Derrick started, but the medic didn't wait. He jabbed the needle into Derrick's arm without hesitation.

"OW! What the—?!" Derrick yelped, pulling his arm back as the sting registered. He glared at the medic. "You could've warned me, you—"

"Save it," the medic interrupted, his tone unbothered. "You'll thank me in about ten seconds."

True to the medic's word, the morphine worked quickly. The tension in Derrick's muscles melted away, and the sharpest edges of his pain dulled to a manageable throb. His scowl softened, and he let out a long breath. "Sorry," he apologized to the medic, his voice sheepish. "Didn't mean to yell."

The medic smirked. "You're welcome."

With Lydia's help, Derrick climbed the steps and collapsed into one of the cabin's couches. His breaths were slow and shallow, his body too drained to protest. Lydia knelt beside him, brushing a damp strand of hair from his forehead. "Rest," she whispered, her voice soft and comforting.

Derrick leaned back, his head lolling against the cushioned seat. His eyes drifted to Arabella, seated with a blanket draped around her shoulders. She was quiet, her wide eyes scanning the unfamiliar surroundings, but the hint of safety in her posture gave him a flicker of reassurance.

Lydia slid onto the couch beside him, guiding his head to her lap. Her fingers traced soothing circles against his temple. "We're going home," she whispered.

As the engines roared to life and the plane began its taxi, Derrick finally let his eyes close. The pain was still there, but the relief of having Arabella safe and seeing Lydia with him was enough to pull him into a deep, dreamless sleep.

CHAPTER 23

When the plane touched down at Andrews Air Force Base, the wheels screeched against the tarmac, signaling the end of a harrowing journey. Flashing lights from the line of vehicles illuminated the scene, casting a glow that reflected off the plane's sleek exterior. Cool morning air swept in as Tae cracked open the door, the crispness a welcome reminder that they were home.

At the bottom of the stairs, President Habatian waited with Katherine, who cradled Madeline in her arms. The President's usually commanding demeanor was softened by visible relief, his focus entirely on the plane. Katherine's grip on Madeline tightened as the door fully opened, her gaze darting between the descending figures.

The first out was Lydia, her arm protectively around Arabella. The young girl clung tightly to Lydia's hand, her movements hesitant but her steps steady as she took in the familiar sight of her parents.

Madeline's eyes lit up the moment she saw Lydia. Wriggling excitedly in Katherine's arms, her tiny voice rang out. "Mama! Mama!"

Katherine smiled and gently set Madeline down. The little girl bolted across the tarmac, her giggles echoing against the plane. Lydia crouched low, her arms outstretched as Madeline launched herself into her mother's embrace.

"Hey, sweetheart," Lydia said, her voice thick with emotion as she held Madeline close. Tears welled in her eyes, spilling over as she kissed her daughter's forehead. The warmth of Madeline's small arms around her neck was the salve Lydia hadn't realized she needed.

Nearby, Arabella broke into a run, throwing herself into her parents' waiting arms. Katherine and the President enveloped her in a fierce embrace, their tears flowing freely as they held their daughter. The President pressed his face against Arabella's hair, while Katherine cupped her daughter's face, her words of comfort and love spilling out in a torrent.

Derrick stood at the top of the stairs, his hand gripping the railing for balance. His legs burned with each step as the adrenaline fully ebbed, leaving behind only pain and exhaustion. He paused, watching the reunion below. His heart swelled at the sight of his family safe and whole.

"You planning to stand there all morning or do you need me to give you a push?" Tae asked from behind him, offering a steadying hand as they began their descent.

Derrick managed a small chuckle, his voice hoarse. "Just... taking it in."

When they reached the bottom, the President turned toward them, his expression a mix of gratitude and admiration. "Thank you," he said, stepping forward to shake Tae's hand firmly before turning to Derrick. "You brought her home. Just like you promised."

Derrick gave a faint nod, his voice quiet. "Just doing my job, sir."

The President's eyes flicked to the bandages visible on Derrick's hands and the stiffness in his movements. "You're hurt," he said, concern overtaking his features. "We need to get you to a hospital."

"It's nothing serious," Derrick said, attempting a reassuring smile. But his voice betrayed his exhaustion, and the wince as he shifted his weight didn't go unnoticed.

Lydia, still holding Madeline close, shot him a look that spoke volumes. She turned to the President with a wry smile. "Maybe you can convince him to listen to reason."

The President raised an eyebrow, his tone firm. "She's right. You've done enough, Derrick. Let us take it from here."

Before Derrick could argue, Tae clapped a hand on his shoulder. "No use fighting it, man. Let's get you patched up."

The hospital had become Derrick's reluctant second home over the following weeks. Burns required time, patience, and excruciating care to heal. Each dressing change was a battle, the raw sting of the ointments and bandages testing his resolve. Alongside the grueling burn treatments, Derrick underwent dental repairs for the teeth he had broken during the integration, the sharp twinges from the procedures serving as a constant reminder of the ordeal. Physical therapy sessions added to the grueling routine, but Derrick approached them with the same grit that had carried him through countless missions.

The steady rhythm of the hospital felt foreign compared to the chaos of the castle, yet it gave him space to think. He found himself replaying the events—Elena's smirk, Cyrus's chilling words, the gunshots that echoed in his ears. The nightmares came often, flashes of the firefight intruding on sleep.

Lydia and Madeline visited daily, their presence anchoring him. Madeline's giggles echoed in the sterile halls, her drawings of stick-figure families taped to the walls near his bed. Lydia brought him books he rarely opened, more intent on hearing her voice than reading the words.

One afternoon, as he stared out the window at the snow-dusted trees, Lydia walked in carrying two cups of coffee. She set one on the table beside him and perched on the edge of the bed.

"You're quiet today," she said, watching him closely.

Derrick exhaled, his hand resting on the bandaged side of his chest. "Just... ready to be home."

"You will be. Soon." Lydia's hand found his, her grip firm. "But promise me, no more playing hero. At least not for a while."

A faint smirk tugged at his lips. "No promises."

She sighed, shaking her head, but her smile betrayed her amusement. "Stubborn as ever."

As Derrick zipped his duffel bag, his phone buzzed on the side table. He glanced at the screen, the President's name flashing. His brow furrowed as he swiped to answer. "Mr. President," he said, his voice pleasant despite his lingering exhaustion.

"Derrick," the President replied, his tone warm but carrying an undertone of gravity. "Before you head home, I'd like you and Lydia to stop by the White House. There's something I want to give you both. Can you be here at noon?"

Derrick hesitated, his grip tightening on the phone. "Understood, sir," he finally said, his voice measured.

Lowering the phone, Derrick glanced at Lydia, who was folding Madeline's sweater nearby. "What was that about?" she asked.

"The President wants us at the White House," Derrick replied, slinging the bag over his shoulder. He didn't elaborate, but Lydia caught the flicker of uncertainty in his eyes.

The White House stood majestic against the winter sky as their SUV pulled up to the entrance. Derrick stepped out first, his legs stiff but functional. The familiar grandeur of the halls greeted them as they were led toward the East Room.

When they entered, Derrick's eyes immediately caught the rows of chairs and the gathered press. Tae stood at the front, dressed in a suit. His posture uncharacteristically reserved. Derrick's heart quickened. This wasn't just a meeting.

The President entered moments later with CIA Director Foster at his side. The room quieted as he approached the podium. His expression carried both pride and solemnity as he began to speak.

"As a nation, we are blessed to have individuals willing to face extraordinary risks for the greater good," the President began, his gaze sweeping the room. "Today, we honor three such individuals—three heroes—whose bravery and sacrifice saved a life and reminded us all of what true service looks like."

Derrick listened intently, but his thoughts drifted to the mission. The crack of gunfire, the acrid stench of smoke, Elena's betrayal, and the way Lydia had cradled Arabella tightly as they fled the chaos. His chest tightened as the memories played like a reel in his mind.

The President motioned for Director Foster, who stepped forward, a box in her hands. She approached Tae first, placing the Distinguished

Intelligence Cross around his neck as she read the commendation text. Tae inclined his head slightly, his usually sharp eyes softening as the room erupted in applause.

The President turned to Lydia. "Lydia Anderson," he said, his voice warm, "your courage under fire and unwavering determination exemplify the very best of us." He presented her with the Presidential Citizens Medal, the applause swelling as Lydia accepted it gratefully. She glanced at Derrick, her pride shining through the tears in her eyes.

Finally, the President faced Derrick. "Derrick Anderson," he began. "Your service to this country transcends any single mission. You have not only defended us, but inspired us. For your bravery, sacrifice, and unwavering dedication, it is my honor to present you with the Presidential Medal of Freedom with Distinction—the highest civilian award of our nation."

The weight of the medal around Derrick's neck felt heavier than it should. As the applause thundered around him, he allowed himself a rare moment of pride, though the memories of those lost along the way tempered it. He glanced at Lydia, and their eyes met. Her gaze was filled with pride and emotion, as though she saw not just the man standing before the crowd, but the man who had carried the weight of so much and still stood strong. She offered him a tender, heartfelt smile that seemed to say, *"You've always been my hero."*

As the ceremony wound down and the press started to disperse, the President approached, extending his hand once more. "You've earned this, Derrick. You all have. We can never truly repay what you've done."

Derrick offered a faint smile, but as the President moved on to Tae, something felt off. Auras formed around everyone's faces and the background noise started fading away. His chest tightened and his vision blurred slightly as he reached for Lydia's arm.

"Derrick?" Lydia's voice was tinged with concern, her hand gripping his elbow.

Before he could respond, a sharp pain shot through his head, and his knees buckled. He collapsed, his body convulsing violently. Lydia's gasp cut through the air like a knife. "Derrick!" she cried, dropping to her knees beside him.

Tae and the President rushed to his side, but the seizure had overtaken him. His muscles contracted and released in rapid spasms, his head jerking against Lydia's lap. Medical staff rushed into the room as reporters froze, unsure of what was happening.

Lydia cradled his head, her voice trembling. "Derrick, stay with me," she pleaded, her words barely audible over the chaos. Tears streamed down her face as she looked up at Tae. "Do something!"

Tae knelt, his voice sharp and commanding as he directed the medics. "Get a stretcher, now!"

CHAPTER 24

The blurred haze of confusion gradually lifted, replaced by the sterile surroundings of an ambulance. The rumble of the vehicle's engine vibrated through him, each jolt on the uneven streets jarring his already aching body. He blinked against the harsh overhead light, his vision swimming as he tried to focus. A medic leaned over him, shining a small flashlight into his eyes.

"Pupils responsive," the medic said to his partner before turning again to Derrick. "Welcome back, sir. How are you feeling?"

Derrick's throat felt dry, his voice rough as he croaked, "What... what happened?"

The lead medic adjusted the IV line attached to his arm. "You had a seizure, sir. We're on the way to George Washington University Hospital. Just try to relax—we'll be there shortly."

A seizure? Derrick's mind scrambled to piece together the fractured timeline. The White House. The ceremony. The medal. Then nothing. It all felt distant, like a dream slipping away upon waking. He let out a strained chuckle, though the sound lacked humor. "GWH? I just left that place. They're going to think I moved in."

The medic cracked a small smile but stayed professional.

"Where's Lydia? And Madeline?" he asked, his voice cracking with concern.

The medic glanced at him with a reassuring look. "They're right behind us. The Secret Service is bringing them. Just rest now, sir."

Derrick shifted slightly, his sore muscles protesting as he looked out the back window. Sure enough, a black SUV followed closely behind, its blue and red lights flashing. The sight brought him a small measure of comfort.

As the ambulance maneuvered through the congested streets of Washington, D.C., Derrick closed his eyes against the pounding in his head. The seizure had left his mind foggy and spinning. The steady beep of the heart monitor and the quiet voices of the medics created a strange sort of white noise that helped calm him.

Derrick winced as the gurney was unloaded, the cold air biting against his skin before the sliding doors of the ER whisked him into warmth.

Doctors and nurses moved quickly to assess his condition. Electrodes were attached to his chest, blood was drawn, and a flurry of medical jargon passed over him like static. Derrick focused on keeping his breathing steady, the lingering haze of the seizure still tugging at the edges of his mind.

One of the nurses, a young woman with a friendly smile, glanced down at him while placing the blood pressure cuff around his arm. Her eyes widened slightly, recognition dawning. "Wait a second," she said, her voice tinged with excitement. "You're Derrick Anderson, aren't you? The guy who saved the President's daughter?"

Derrick blinked, caught off guard. "Uh, yeah. That's me."

The nurse grinned, tightening the cuff. "I knew it! My dad's ex-military—he never shuts up about you. Always saying how you're a legend." Her tone became playful. "You know, you're even more handsome in person."

Derrick let out a soft chuckle, though it turned into a wince as the cuff inflated. "Flattery's nice and all, but I'm not sure my heart rate needs any more encouragement right now."

The nurse laughed, brushing her hair back. "Well, if you ever get tired of saving the world, I know a good coffee shop in Georgetown."

Before Derrick could respond, the door to the room opened, and Lydia stepped inside. Her eyes immediately locked onto him, concern etched into her face. The nurse's gaze flicked to Lydia, her expression shifting as realization set in.

Lydia approached the bed, her hand instinctively reaching out to touch Derrick's shoulder. "How is he?" she asked.

The nurse smiled, stepping back to give her space. "Stable and in good hands," she said, her tone still light. She turned back to Derrick, a teasing smile on her lips. "Well, I never had a chance, did I?"

Derrick gave a faint grin, his gaze shifting to Lydia. "Sorry, not even close," he replied, the sincerity in his voice clear.

The nurse laughed, gathering her supplies. "He's all yours, Mrs. Anderson," she said, giving Lydia a friendly smile before stepping out of the room.

Lydia raised an eyebrow at Derrick, a hint of amusement breaking through her worry. "Making friends already?"

Derrick chuckled softly, though the movement made his chest ache. "What can I say? I'm irresistible."

Lydia shook her head, leaning down to kiss his forehead. "Just focus on getting better, Romeo."

Madeline peeked around the doorway, and Lydia motioned her inside. As the little girl climbed onto the bed to hug her father, Derrick let out a content sigh. For the first time in what felt like forever, he allowed himself to simply be present, surrounded by the people who mattered most.

After what felt like an eternity of tests, Derrick was wheeled into a private room. The overhead fluorescent lights had been dimmed, casting a softer glow over the sterile environment. But the true source of comfort wasn't the room—it was Lydia and Madeline waiting for him.

She rose from the chair by the window, her face lighting up with relief and concern as she crossed the room. "Hey," she said softly, her hand brushing against his cheek.

Derrick managed a weak smile, his voice raspier than he intended. "Guess I know how to make an exit, huh? Sorry for the drama."

Lydia's lips twitched into a faint smile, but her eyes betrayed the worry she carried. "Derrick, don't," she said, her voice trembling slightly. "You scared me."

The weight of her words hit him like a blow. She had every right to feel this way. He had put her through so much, and now this. His attempt at humor had been to lighten her load, but it was clear she wasn't ready for that yet.

"I'm sorry," he whispered, his fingers brushing against hers. "It's probably just stress. Nothing serious."

Lydia knelt beside him, her eyes searching his face. "Stress doesn't cause seizures, Derrick," she explained. "We'll figure it out. But you're not doing this alone."

Before he could respond, a small head peeked over the side of the bed. Madeline climbed up with Lydia's help, her tiny arms wrapping around his chest. "Daddy," she said, her voice muffled against his hospital gown. "No more getting hurt."

He chuckled weakly, stroking her hair. "I'll do my best, peanut."

Lydia leaned down, pressing a kiss to his temple. "We're here," she said softly, her voice carrying a quiet strength. "All of us."

The soft rhythm of Derrick's breathing filled the hospital room as he slept. Madeline had curled up beside him, her tiny hand resting on his bandaged arm. Lydia sat in the chair beside them, her fingers lightly brushing through Madeline's hair as she watched her husband and daughter. This quiet moment felt both a blessing and a cruel pause—time to reflect on the weight of everything they had been through.

A knock at the door broke the stillness, and Lydia turned to see the doctor entering the room, a chart in hand and an expression that carried both professionalism and gravity. Derrick stirred at the sound, blinking awake.

"Mr. Anderson, Mrs. Anderson," the doctor began, stepping closer. "We've reviewed your scans and consulted with a neurologist. I'd like to go over your findings."

Derrick raised the bed some as not to disturb Madeline. Lydia leaned forward, her hand instinctively finding his.

The doctor took a deep breath before continuing. "We found a tumor in the parietal lobe of your brain. The good news is that it's benign—it's not cancerous. However, its location makes it inoperable.

It's deeply embedded, and while we can manage the symptoms, surgery isn't an option."

The words hung in the air like a heavy weight. Derrick's jaw tightened, but his face portrayed no fear, only quiet contemplation. Lydia, on the other hand, gripped his hand tighter, her mind racing.

"How long do I have?" Derrick asked, his voice calm but edged with tension.

The doctor shook his head gently. "It's difficult to say. This type of tumor can sometimes be managed for years, even decades. But the symptoms you're experiencing—like the seizures—may worsen over time. We'll need to monitor it closely and begin treatment to manage the symptoms."

Lydia's voice broke the silence, her tone calm despite the turmoil inside. "What kind of treatment?"

"Anti-seizure medication, physical therapy if the motor issues progress, and regular scans to monitor the tumor's growth. Stress will need to be minimized as much as possible," the doctor said, his gaze shifting between them. "Mr. Anderson, I know your career has been demanding, but it's vital you take steps to reduce physical strain and emotional stress."

Derrick nodded, though his expression remained inscrutable. "Understood."

The doctor's gaze softened as he turned to Lydia. "He'll need your support to make these changes. And if there's anything else we can do to help, please let us know."

As the doctor left, the weight of his words settled over them. Lydia turned to Derrick, brushing her fingers lightly over his hand. "We'll get through this," she whispered.

He gave her a faint smile, though his eyes betrayed the storm behind them. "We've made it through worse. I'm sure I'll be fine," he said, though his confidence faded and was replaced with worry.

Later, as the hours passed, Derrick managed to sit up, his strength slowly returning. When Tae arrived, Derrick's face lit up, his usual humor shining through despite the circumstances.

"Tae," Derrick said, his voice carrying a playful edge. "Come to check on the cripple?"

Tae smirked, crossing his arms as he leaned against the doorframe. "Nah, just came to make sure you haven't turned the hospital into a war zone yet."

Lydia couldn't help but smile as Tae sat beside Derrick, the two of them falling into an easy rhythm of banter. They talked about old missions, shared jokes, and even teased Lydia about her ability to outmaneuver both of them in a tactical simulation years ago.

For a little while, the room felt lighter, the heaviness of Derrick's condition pushed to the background. Lydia watched the two friends, her heart aching with gratitude for Tae's presence. He had always been a grounding force for Derrick—a brother in every way that mattered.

When it was time for Tae to leave, Lydia stood to walk him out. As they stepped into the cool night air, the weight she had been holding in began to surface. Her steps faltered, and Tae immediately turned to her.

"Lydia?" he asked softly, his brow rising with concern.

She shook her head, her voice breaking as the tears finally spilled over. "I don't know how to do this, Tae. How do I make him slow down? How do I stop being terrified that every day could be the day I lose him?"

Tae didn't hesitate. He pulled her into a tight hug. "You don't have to do it alone," he said quietly. "You've got me. This isn't going to beat you. Just tell me what you need."

Lydia pulled back slightly, her tear-filled eyes meeting his. "There is one thing," she said softly, her voice trembling but determined. "Promise me you'll keep him out of the field. If he tries to push himself... if he tries to go back to what he was doing before—"

Tae cut her off with a solemn nod. "You have my word. Whatever it takes, I'll make sure he doesn't do anything stupid."

A faint smile broke through her tears. "That's a tall order."

He gave her a lopsided grin. "Hey, stupid is my specialty. Derrick's just an amateur." The humor worked—Lydia let out a soft laugh, shaking her head.

"Thank you, Tae," she said, her voice steadier now.

"Always," he replied, his tone filled with quiet certainty.

***

The last few days had passed in a haze of recovery, filled with moments of quiet reflection and healing. Derrick's strength was returning slowly but steadily, though he was keenly aware of how much he still had to overcome.

As they packed up their belongings, preparing to leave the hospital, Derrick felt an odd mixture of relief and apprehension.

Madeline's soft giggles floated through the room as she played by the window, her innocent laughter acting as a soothing balm. He sat on the edge of the hospital bed watching Lydia help Madeline place toys into her bag. It was a reminder of everything he had to fight for. His chest still ached, and his legs burned faintly with every movement, but he was alive, and they were together. That was enough.

But as Lydia moved quietly around the room, he could feel her nervous energy, the way her gaze lingered on him when she thought he wasn't looking. Something was on her mind. He was about to ask when a knock at the door interrupted. It was Tae.

Stepping inside, his expression was more serious than normal. Derrick straightened slightly, sensing the shift in the room. "Hey, Buddy," he greeted with curiosity. "What's up?"

Tae glanced at Lydia before meeting Derrick's gaze. Stepping closer, he sighed. "Derrick, we need to talk."

The tension in the room thickened. Lydia froze, her hand clutching the strap of the overnight bag she was packing. Tilting his head, Derrick studied his friend. "Go on," he said, his voice cautious.

Tae exhaled slowly, then spoke. "We've reviewed everything—your medical status, the last mission, the risks you've taken. The decision's been made, Derrick. Your overseas clearance is revoked. Your contractor status is terminated. Effective immediately, you're relieved of active duty."

The words hit like a physical blow. Derrick blinked, his mind racing to catch up. He had known this day would come... eventually. But to hear it now, after everything—after the medals, the mission, and the fight—it was like the ground had been pulled out from under him.

Lydia's hand rested on his shoulder, comforting him. Glancing up at her, he saw the worry in her eyes. She already knew.

Of course she did.

Derrick turned his gaze back to Tae, who continued, his voice softer now. "Your country owes you everything, Derrick. You've given more than anyone could ask. But it's time to focus on what matters. Go home. Be with Lydia. Be with Madeline. You've earned that."

Derrick's chest tightened, a flood of emotions welling up inside him—grief, anger, relief, and, strangely... gratitude. For years, his life had been dictated by missions, by the call to serve. But now, the choice was being taken from him, and as much as it stung, he realized it was for the best. He wasn't just a soldier or a contractor. He was a husband, a father. And it was time to be those things fully.

He swallowed hard. "Thank you, Tae," he said, extending a hand to his friend.

Tae took it, gripping it firmly. There was nothing more to say—no words that could capture the history they shared or the weight of this moment.

As Tae left the room, Lydia moved to Derrick's side, her gaze searching his face. "You're okay with this?" she asked softly.

Derrick exhaled, a faint smile touching his lips as he met her eyes. "I think I am," he said. His voice was tinged with acceptance—and maybe even a hint of peace. "It's time."

Lydia's eyes filled with tears, and she wrapped her arms around him, holding him tightly. "Thank you," she whispered, her voice trembling with emotion.

***

As they pulled into their driveway, Derrick leaned back in his seat, letting out a long, slow breath. The familiar outline of their home stood against the sunset glowing sky, its porch light casting a warm, inviting glow. For the first time in what felt like years, the weight he carried didn't feel so heavy. It wasn't just the end of a chapter—it was the beginning of something new.

Lydia glanced over at him, her hand resting lightly on his arm. "Ready?" she asked softly.

He met her gaze, his lips curving into a faint smile. "Never been readier."

Madeline stirred in her booster seat, her sleepy eyes blinking as she looked up. "Are we home?" she murmured, her voice thick with drowsiness.

Lydia turned to her daughter, smoothing a hand over her hair. "We are, sweetheart."

Derrick glanced at Lydia, his eyes meeting hers with a longing she hadn't seen in years. "To stay."

As they got out of the vehicle, the sound of laughter and the clatter of dishes drifted from the house. The front door swung open, and Mary appeared, her apron dusted with flour, a wide smile spreading across her face. "There you are!" she called, wiping her hands on the apron as she stepped onto the porch. "I've got dinner almost ready—roast chicken, mashed potatoes, green beans, and pie for dessert."

Jeb's voice rumbled from the living room, where the faint drone of the Weather Channel carried through the open window. "And don't forget the rolls! The boy deserves something good after what he's been through!"

Derrick chuckled as he hefted his duffel bag over his shoulder, the ache in his chest and legs fading in the warmth of the moment. "You spoil me, Jeb," he called back, his voice light with amusement.

"Someone's gotta," Jeb replied, his grin audible even if his face wasn't visible.

Stepping inside, the aroma of home-cooked food wrapped around them like a comforting embrace. Mary bustled back to the kitchen, and Jeb smirked as he gave a lazy wave from the recliner. "Weather's looking good," he said, gesturing to the TV. "Figured you'd want to know."

Derrick dropped his bag by the door, sinking onto the couch with a groan. "You're too kind," he drawled, the humor in his voice masking his deep appreciation.

Lydia appeared from the hallway, carrying a bundle of fresh clothes for Madeline, who had already begun pulling off her shoes. She paused when she saw Derrick leaning back, his eyes closed and head tilted against the cushion.

"You doing okay over there?" she teased, her tone light but carrying a thread of genuine concern.

Derrick cracked an eye open, a mischievous glint sparking. "I was just thinking," he said, sitting up slightly. "Maybe it's time to take that job offer from the community college."

Lydia's eyes widened, her lips twitching with intrigue. "The community college? Doing what?"

"Teaching," he replied casually, leaning back again.

"Teaching what?" she pressed, narrowing her eyes suspiciously.

Derrick's smirk widened, his tone deliberately nonchalant. "Chemistry."

The realization hit her like a freight train. She groaned loudly, dropping her head into her hands. "Oh, dear Lord, no!" she exclaimed, her voice muffled but unmistakably dramatic.

Jeb barked out a laugh from his recliner, and even Mary peeked out from the kitchen with a raised eyebrow. Derrick laughed, the sound rich and unrestrained, a rare moment of pure joy.

"What?" he asked, feigning innocence. "I thought you'd be proud."

Lydia lifted her head and gave him a look of mock horror. "Derrick, the world doesn't need you blowing up a lab full of unsuspecting students."

"They'd learn faster that way," he countered with a grin.

Shaking her head, Lydia walked over and plopped down beside him, her shoulder pressing into his. "You're impossible."

"And you love me for it," he said, his grin softening as he turned to her.

She smiled, leaning her head against his shoulder. "I really do."

As Mary called them to the table, Derrick wrapped an arm around Lydia, pulling her closer.

Madeline's laughter filled the room, blending with the gentle hum of conversation and Jeb's cheerful commentary about the weather. For the first time in a long while, Derrick felt something he hadn't dared to believe in: peace.

This wasn't just a house or a place to rest—it was a haven, a reminder of how blessed he was.

He turned to Lydia, her smile soft and full of happiness, and then to Madeline, whose sleepy giggle broke through the quiet. This was his home. His future.

And for once, the fight was over.